2—

THIRTY-SIX MILES

"For the first time he felt unbearably hot—with a heat that contributed to his mounting fury. The morning's sun began to flagellate him anew, adding curious sharp blades of pain to the furious frustration boiling inside him. Frustration at the fact that he . . . was not *man* enough to say, to hell with it and crap himself out; that he was not man enough to disavow his determination and endurance and suffering, cash in his chips, and by that act flaunt his contempt of the march, the Colonel, the whole bloody Marine Corps. But he was *not* man enough, he knew, far less simply a free man; he was just a marine . . ."

THE LONG MARCH

William Styron

BANTAM BOOKS
TORONTO • NEW YORK • LONDON

*This low-priced Bantam Book
has been completely reset in a type face
designed for easy reading, and was printed
from new plates. It contains the complete
text of the original hard-cover edition.*
NOT ONE WORD HAS BEEN OMITTED.

THE LONG MARCH

*A Bantam Book / published by arrangement with
Random House, Inc.*

PRINTING HISTORY

*Bantam Windstone edition / June 1981
2nd printing . . . October 1983*

*Random House edition published March 1968
2 printings through March 1980*

*This title was included in a Four Volume Set Selection
by Book-of-the-Month Club July 1979.*

*Windstone and accompanying logo of a stylized W
are trademarks of Bantam Books, Inc.*

*Bantam Books are published by Bantam Books, Inc. Its trade-
mark, consisting of the words "Bantam Books" and the portrayal of a rooster, is Registered in U.S. Patent and Trademark
Office and in other countries. Marca Registrada. Bantam
Books, Inc., 666 Fifth Avenue, New York, New York 10103.*

PRINTED IN THE UNITED STATES OF AMERICA

H   11 10 9 8 7 6 5 4 3 2

To Hiram Haydn

William Styron

THE LONG MARCH

ONE

One noon, in the blaze of a cloudless Carolina summer, what was left of eight dead boys lay strewn about the landscape, among the poison ivy and the pine needles and loblolly saplings. It was not so much as if they had departed this life but as if, sprayed from a hose, they were only shreds of bone, gut, and dangling tissue to which it would have been impossible ever to impute the quality of life, far less the capacity to relinquish it. Of course, though, these had really died quickly, no doubt before the faintest flicker of recognition, of wonder, apprehension, or terror had had time to register in their minds. But the shock, it occurred to Lieutenant Culver, who stood in the shady lee of an ambulance and watched the scene, must have been fantastic to those on the periphery of the explosion, those fifteen or so surviving marines who now lay on the ground beneath blankets, moaning with pain and fright, and who, not more than half

1

an hour before, had been waiting patiently in line for their lunch before the two mortar shells, misfired—how? why? the question already hung with a buzzing, palpable fury in the noontime heat— had plummeted down upon the chow-line and had deadened their ears and senses and had hurled them earthward where they lay now, alive but stricken in a welter of blood and brain, scattered messkits and mashed potatoes, and puddles of melting ice cream. Moments ago in the confusion—just before he had stolen off from the Colonel's side to go behind a tree and get sick—Lieutenant Culver had had a glimpse of a young sweaty face grimed with dust, had heard the boy's voice, astonishing even in that moment of nausea because of its clear, unhysterical tone of explanation: "Major, I tell you I was on the field phone and I tell you as soon as they come out the tube I knew they were short rounds and so I hollered . . ." Of course it had been an accident. But why? He heard the Major shout something; then Culver had heard no more, retching on the leaves with a sound that, for a moment, drowned out the cries and whines of the wounded and the noise of trucks and ambulances crashing up through the underbrush.

It was not that he had a weak stomach or that he was unacquainted with carnage that allowed him to lose control. If anything, he prided himself on his stomach, and as for the blood he had seen a lot spilled on Okinawa and had himself (although through no act of valor whatever) received a shrapnel wound—in the buttocks, a matter which even in retrospect, as he had often been forced to remind his wife, possessed no elements of comedy at all. In

2

this case it was simply that on the one hand he himself had been shocked. The sight of death was the sort of thing which in wartime is expected, which one protects oneself against, and which is finally excused or at least ignored, in the same way that a beggar is ignored, or a head cold, or a social problem. But in training here in the States in peacetime (or what, this sweltering summer in the early 1950s, passed as peacetime) one had felt no particular need for that type of self-defense, and the slick nude litter of intestine and shattered blue bones, among which forks and spoons peeked out like so many pathetic metal flowers, made a crazy, insulting impact at Culver's belly, like the blow of a fist. And on the other hand (and the pulsing ache at his brow now as he vomited helplessly onto his shoes lent confirmation to what he'd been trying to deny to himself for months): he was too old, he was no longer an eager kid just out of Quantico with a knife between his teeth. He was almost thirty, he was old, and he was afraid.

Lieutenant Culver had been called back to the marines early that spring. When, one Saturday morning, his wife had thrown the brown envelope containing his orders onto the bed where he lay sleeping, he experienced an odd distress which kept him wandering about, baffled and mumbling to himself, for days. Like most of his fellow reserves he had retained his commission after the last war. It was an insouciant gesture which he had assumed would in some way benefit him in case of an all-out conflict, say, thirty years hence, but one which made no provisions for such an eventuality as a police action in Korea. It had all come much too soon and Culver

3

had felt weirdly as if he had fallen asleep in some barracks in 1945 and had awakened in a half-dozen years or so to find that the intervening freedom, growth, and serenity had been only a glorious if somewhat prolonged dream. A flood of protest had welled up in him, for he had put the idea of war out of his mind entirely, and the brief years since Okinawa had been the richest of his life. They had produced, among lesser things, a loving, tenderly passionate wife who had passed on to their little girl both some of her gentle nature and her wealth of butter-colored hair; a law degree, the fruits of which he had just begun to realize, even though still somewhat impecuniously, as one of the brightest juniors in a good New York law firm; a friendly beagle named Howard whom he took for hikes in Washington Square; a cat, whom he did not deign to call by name, and despised; and a record-player that played Haydn, Mozart and Bach.

Up until the day that his orders came—the day that he tried to forget and the one that Betsy, his wife, soon bitterly referred to as "the day the roof fell in"—they had been living in a roomy walk-up in the Village and experiencing the prosaic contentment that comes from eating properly, indulging themselves with fair moderation in the pleasures of the city, and watching the growth of a child. This is not to say that they were either smug or dull. They had a bright circle of friends, mostly young lawyers and newspapermen and doctors and their wives. There were parties and occasional week ends in the country, where everyone became frankly drunk. There were the usual household skirmishes, too, but these were infrequent and petered out

4

quickly. Both of them were too sensible to allow
some domestic misdemeanor to develop into anything horrible; they were well adjusted and each of
them found it easy to admit, long after the honey-
moon, that they were deeply in love. Months later
at camp, ensnared futilely in the coils of some ad-
ministrative flypaper, Culver would find himself
gazing up from his work and out across the smoky
hot barrens of pine and sand, relieving his vast
boredom in a daydream of that vanished simplicity
and charm. His mind seemed to drift toward one
recurrent vision. This was of the afternoons in
winter when—bundled to the ears, the baby-car-
riage joggling bravely in the van and the melan-
choly beagle scampering at their heels—they took
their Sunday stroll. On such days the city, its frantic
heartbeat quieted and clothed in the sooty white
tatters of a recent snow, seemed to have an Old
World calm, and the people that passed them in the
twilight appeared to be, like themselves, pink-
cheeked and contented, no matter what crimson
alarms flowered at the newsstands or what evil
rumors sounded from distant radios. For Culver the
waning Sunday light had not spelled out the promise of Monday morning's gloom but of Monday's
challenge—and this was not because he was a go-
getter but because he was happy. He was happy to
walk through the chill and leafless dusk with his
wife and his child and his dog. And he was happy to
return home to warmth and peanut butter and liver-
wurst, to the familiar delight of the baby's good-
night embrace, to the droll combat between beagle
and cat, to music before sleep. Sometimes in these
reveries Culver thought that it was the music, more

than anything, which provided the key, and he recalled himself at a time which already seemed dark
ages ago, surrounded by beer cans and attuned, in
the nostalgic air of a winter evening, to some passage from some forgotten Haydn. It was one happy
and ascending bar that he remembered, a dozen
bright notes through which he passed in memory
to an earlier, untroubled day at the end of child-
hood. There, like tumbling flowers against the sunny grass, their motions as nimble as the music itself,
two lovely little girls played tennis, called to him
voicelessly, as in a dream, and waved their arms.

The sordid little town outside the camp possessed the horror of recognition, for Culver had
been there before. They left the baby with a sister
and headed south where, on the outskirts of the
town, they found a cramped room in a tourist cabin.
They were there for two weeks. They searched
vainly for a place to live, there was no more room
at the camp. They turned away from bleak cell-like
rooms offered at five times their value, were shown
huts and chicken-coops by characters whose bland
country faces could not hide the sparkle, in their
calculating eyes, of venal lust. The aging proprie-
tress of the tourist camp was a scold and a cheat.
And so they finally gave up. Betsy went home. He
kissed her good-by late one rainy afternoon in the
bus station, surrounded by a horde of marines and
by cheap suitcases and fallen candy wrappers and
the sound of fretful children—all of the unlovely
mementoes, so nightmarishly familiar, of leave-
taking and of anxiety. Of war. He felt her tears
against his cheek. It had been an evil day, and the
rain that streamed against the windows, blurring a

distant frieze of gaunt gray pines, had seemed to nag with both remembrance and foreboding—of tropic seas, storm-swept distances and strange coasts.

TWO

He had heard the explosion himself. They had been eating at their own chow-line in a command post set up in a grove of trees, when the noise came from off to the right, distant enough but still too close: a twin quick earthshaking sound—*crump crump*. Then seconds later in the still of noon when even the birds had become quiet and only a few murmured voices disturbed the concentration of eating, a shudder had passed through the surrounding underbrush, like a faint hot wind. It was premonitory, perhaps, but still no one knew. The leaves rustled, ceased, and Culver had looked up from where he squatted against a tree to see fifty scattered faces peering toward the noise, their knives and forks suspended. Then from the galley among the trees a clatter broke the silence, a falling pan or kettle, and someone laughed, and the Colonel, sitting nearby, had said to the Major— what had he said? Culver couldn't remember, yet

8

there had been something uneasy in his tone, even
then, before anyone had known, and at least ten
minutes before the radio corporal, a tobacco-chew-
ing clown from Oklahoma named Hobbs, came trot-
ting up brushing crumbs from his mouth, a message
book clutched in one fat paw. He was popular in
battalion headquarters, one of those favored men
who, through some simplicity or artlessness of nature, can manage a profane familiarity which in
another would be insubordinate; the look of con-
cern on his clown's face, usually so whimsical, com-
municated an added dread.

"I gotta flash red from Plumbob, Colonel, and
it ain't no problem emergency. All hell's broke loose
over in Third Battalion. They dropped in some short
rounds on a chow-line and they want corpsmen and
a doctor and the chaplain. Jesus, you should hear
'em down there."

The Colonel had said nothing at first. The brief
flicker of uneasiness in his eyes had fled, and when
he put down his messkit and looked up at Hobbs
it was only to wipe his hands on his handkerchief
and squint casually into the sun, as if he were re-
ceiving the most routine of messages. It was abso-
lutely typical of the man, Culver reflected. Too
habitual to be an act yet still somehow too faintly
self-conscious to be entirely natural, how many
years and what strange interior struggle had gone
into the perfection of such a gesture? It was good,
Grade-A Templeton, perhaps not a distinctly top-
notch performance but certainly, from where the
critic Culver sat, deserving of applause: the frail,
little-boned, almost pretty face peering upward
with a look of attitudinized contemplation; the

9

pensive bulge of tongue sliding inside the rim of one tanned cheek to gouge out some particle of food; small hands working calmly in the folds of the handkerchief—surely all this was more final, more commanding than the arrogant loud mastery of a Booth, more like the skill of Bernhardt, who could cow men by the mystery of her smallest twitch. Perhaps fifteen seconds passed before he spoke. Culver became irritated—at his own suspense, throbbing inside him like a heartbeat, and at the awesome silence which, as if upon order, had fallen over the group of five, detached from the bustle of the rest of the command post: the Colonel; Hobbs; Major Lawrence, the executive officer, now gazing at the Colonel with moist underlip and deferential anxiety; Captain Mannix; himself. Back off in the bushes a mockingbird commenced a shrill rippling chant and far away, amidst the depth of the silence, there seemed to be a single faint and terrible scream. Hobbs spat an auburn gob of tobacco-juice into the sand, and the Colonel spoke: "Let me have that radio, Hobbs, and get me Plumbob One," he said evenly, and then with no change of tone to the Major: "Billy, send a runner over for Doc Patterson and you two get down there with the chaplain. Take my jeep. Tell the Doc to detach all his corpsmen. And you'd better chop-chop."

The Major scrambled to his feet. He was youthful and handsome, a fine marine in his polished boots, his immaculate dungarees—donned freshly clean, Culver had observed, that morning. He was of the handsomeness preferred by other military men—regular features, clean-cut, rather athletic—

but there was a trace of peacetime fleshiness in
his cheeks which often lent to the corners of his
mouth a sort of petulance, so that every now and
again, his young uncomplicated face in deep concentration over some operations map or training
schedule or order, he looked like a spoiled and
arrogant baby of five. "Aye-aye, sir," he said and
bent over the Colonel, bestowing upon him that
third-person flattery which to Culver seemed per-
ilously close to bootlicking and was thought to be
considerably out of date, especially among the
reserves. "Does the Colonel want us to run our own
problem as ordered, sir?" He was a regular.

Templeton took the headset from Hobbs, who
lowered the radio down beside him in the sand.
"Yeah, Billy," he said, without looking up, "yeah,
that'll be all right. We'll run her on time. Tell
O'Leary to tell all companies to push off at thirteen
hundred."

"Aye-aye, sir." And the Major, boots sparkling,
was off in a puff of pine needles and dust.

"Jesus," Mannix said. He put down his messkit
and nudged Culver in the ribs. Captain Mannix,
the commanding officer of headquarters company,
was Culver's friend and, for five months, his closest
one. He was a dark heavy-set Jew from Brooklyn,
Culver's age and a reserve, too, who had had to
sell his radio store and leave his wife and two
children at home. He had a disgruntled sense of
humor which often seemed to bring a spark of
relief not just to his own, but to Culver's, feeling
of futility and isolation. Mannix was a bitter man and,
in his bitterness, sometimes recklessly vocal. He
had long ago given up genteel accents, and spoke

11

like a marine. It was easier, he maintained. "Je-*sus*," he whispered again, too loud, "what'll Congress do about this? Look at Billy chop-chop."

Culver said nothing. His tension eased off a bit, and he looked around him. The news had not seemed yet to have spread around the command post; the men began to get up and walk to the chow-line to clean their messgear, strolled back beneath the trees and flopped down, heads against their packs, for a moment's nap. The Colonel spoke in an easy, confidential voice with the other battalion commander: the casualties were confined, Culver gathered, to that outfit. It was a battalion made up mostly of young reserves and it was one in which, he suddenly thanked God, he knew no one. Then he heard the Colonel go on calmly—to promise more aid, to promise to come down himself, shortly. "Does it look rough, Luke?" Culver heard him say, "Hold on tight, Luke boy"—all in the cool and leisurely, almost bored, tones of a man to whom the greatest embarrassment would be a show of emotion, and to whom, because of this quality, had been given, in the midst of some strained and violent combat situation long ago, the name "Old Rocky." He was not yet forty-five, yet the adjective "old" applied, for there was a gray sheen in his hair and a bemused, unshakable look in his tranquil eyes that made him seem, like certain young ecclesiastics, prematurely aged and perhaps even wise. Culver saw him put the headset down and get up, walking off toward the operations tent with a springy, slim-hipped, boyish stride, calling out over his shoulder as he went: "Mannix." Simply that: Mannix. A voice neither harsh nor

peremptory nor, on the other hand, particularly
gentle. It was merely a voice which expected to
be obeyed, and Culver felt Mannix's big weight
against him as the Captain put a hand on his shoulder and pried himself up from the ground, muttering, "Jesus, lemme digest a bit, Jack."

Mannix despised the Colonel. Yet, Culver
thought, as the Captain hulked stiff-kneed behind
the Colonel and disappeared after him into the
operations tent, Mannix despised everything about
the Marine Corps. In this attitude he was like
nearly all the reserves, it was true, but Mannix was
more noisily frank in regard to his position. He
detested Templeton not because of any slight or
injustice, but because Templeton was a lieutenant
colonel, because he was a regular, and because he
possessed over Mannix—after six years of freedom
—an absolute and unquestioned authority. Mannix
would have hated any battalion commander, had he
the benignity of Santa Claus, and Culver, listening
to Mannix's frequently comical but often too audible complaints, as just now, was kept in a constant
state of mild suspense—half amusement, half horror. Culver settled himself against the tree. Apparently there was nothing, for the moment at least,
that he could do. Above him an airplane droned
through the stillness. A truck grumbled across the
clearing, carrying a group of languid hospital corpsmen, was gone; around him the men lay against
their packs in crumpled attitudes of sleep. A heavy
drowsiness came over him, and he let his eyes slide
closed. Suddenly he yearned, with all of the hunger
of a schoolboy in a classroom on a May afternoon,
to be able to collapse into slumber. For the three

days they had been on the problem he had averaged only four hours of sleep a night—almost none last night—and gratefully he knew he'd be able to sleep this evening. He began to doze, dreaming fitfully of home, of white cottages, of a summer by the sea. *Long walk tonight.* And his eyes snapped open then—on what seemed to be the repeated echo, from afar, of the faint anguished shriek he had heard before—in the horrid remembrance that there would be no sleep tonight. For anyone at all. Only a few seconds had passed.

"Long walk tonight," the voice repeated. Culver stared upward through a dazzling patchwork of leaves and light to see the broad pink face of Sergeant O'Leary, smiling down.

"Christ, O'Leary," he said, "don't remind me."

The Sergeant, still grinning, gestured with his shoulder in the direction of the operations tent. "The Colonel's really got a wild hair, ain't he?" He chuckled and reached down and clutched one of his feet, with an elaborate groan.

Culver abruptly felt cloaked in a gloom that was almost tangible, and he was in no mood to laugh. "You'll be really holding that foot tomorrow morning," he said, "and that's no joke."

The grin persisted. "Ah, Mister Culver," O'Leary said, "don't take it so hard. It's just a little walk through the night. It'll be over before you know it." He paused, prodding with his toe at the pine needles. "Say," he went on, "what's this I heard about some short rounds down in Third Batt?"

"I don't know from nothing, O'Leary. I just read the papers." Another truck came by, loaded with corpsmen, followed by a jeep in which sat the helmeted Major Lawrence, a look of sulky arrogance on his face, his arms folded at his chest like a legionnaire riding through a conquered city. "But from what I understand," Culver went on, turning back, "quite a few guys got hurt."

"That's tough," O'Leary said. "I'll bet you they were using that old stuff they've had stored on Guam ever since '45. Jesus, you'd think they'd have better sense. Why, I seen those shells stacked up high as a man out there just last year, getting rained on every day and getting the jungle rot and Jesus, they put tarps over 'em but five years is one hell of a long time to let 81-shells lay around. I remember once . . ." Culver let him talk, without hearing the words, and drowsed. O'Leary was an old-timer (though only a few years older than Culver), a regular who had just signed over for four more years, and it was impossible to dislike him. On Guadalcanal he had been only a youngster, but in the intervening years the Marine Corps had molded him—perhaps by his own unconscious choice—in its image, and he had become as inextricably grafted to the system as any piece of flesh surgically laid on to arm or thigh. There was great heartiness and warmth in him but at the same time he performed all infantry jobs with a devoted, methodical competence. He could say sarcastically, "The Colonel's really got a wild hair, ain't he?" but shrug his shoulders and grin, and by that ambivalent gesture sum up an attitude which only a professional soldier could logically retain: I doubt the Colonel's judgment a little, but I will willingly do what he says. He also shared with Hobbs, the radioman, some sort of immunity. And thus it had been last night, Culver recalled, that upon the Colonel's announcement about this evening's forced march —which was to take thirteen hours and extend the nearly thirty-six miles back to the main base— O'Leary had been able to give a long, audible, incredulous whistle, right in the Colonel's face, and elicit from the Colonel an indulgent smile; whereas in the same blackout tent and at virtually the same instant Mannix had murmured, "Thirty-six miles, Jesus Christ," in a tone, however, laden with no more disbelief or no more pain than O'Leary's whistle, and Culver had seen the Colonel's smile vanish, replaced on the fragile little face by a subtle, delicate shadow of irritation.

"You think that's too long?" the Colonel had said to Mannix then, turning slightly. There had been no hostility in his voice, or even reproof; it had, in fact, seemed merely a question candidly stated—although this might have been because two enlisted men had been in the tent, O'Leary, and some wizened, anonymous little private shivering over the radio. It was midsummer, but nights out in the swamps were fiercely, illogically cold, and from where they had set up the operations tent that evening—on a tiny patch of squashy marshland—the dampness seemed to ooze up and around them, clutching their bones in a chill which extra sweaters and field jackets and sweatshirts could not dislodge. A single kerosene pressure-lamp dangled from overhead—roaring like a pint-sized, encapsuled hurricane; it furnished the only light in the tent, and the negligible solace of a candlelike light one imagines in an execution chamber; under it the Colonel's face, in absolute repose as he stared down for a brief, silent instant and awaited Mannix's reply, looked like that of a mannequin, chalky, exquisite, solitary beneath a store-window glare.

"No, sir," Mannix said. He had recovered quickly. He peered up at the Colonel from his camp stool, expressionless. "No, sir," he repeated, "I don't think it's too long, but it's certainly going to be some hike."

The Colonel did something with his lips. It seemed to be a smile. He said nothing—bemused and mystifying—wearing the enigma of the moment like a cape. In the silence the tempestuous little lamp boiled and raged; far off in the swamp somewhere a mortar flare flew up with a short, sharp crack. O'Leary broke the quietness in the tent with a loud sneeze, followed, almost like a prolongation of the sneeze, by a chuckle, and said: "Oh boy, Colonel, there're gonna be some sore feet Saturday morning."

The Colonel didn't answer. He hooked his thumbs in his belt. He turned to the Major, who was brooding upward from the field desk, cheeks propped against his hands. "I was sitting in my tent a while ago, Billy," the Colonel said, "and I got to thinking. I got to thinking about a lot of things. I got to thinking about the Battalion. I said to myself, 'How's the Battalion doing?' I mean, 'What kind of an outfit do I have here? Is it in good combat shape? If we were to meet an Aggressor enemy tomorrow would we come out all right?' Those were the queries I posed to myself. Then I tried to formulate an answer." He paused, his eyes luminous and his lips twisted in a wry, contemplative smile as if he were indeed, again, struggling with the weight of

17

the questions to which he had addressed himself. The Major was absorbed; he looked up at Templeton with an intent baby-blue gaze and parted mouth, upon which, against a pink cleft of the lower lip, there glittered a bead of saliva. "Reluctantly," the Colonel went on slowly, "reluctantly, I came to this conclusion: the Battalion's been doping off." He paused again. "Doping off. Especially," he said, turning briefly toward Mannix with a thin smile, "a certain component unit known as Headquarters and Service Company." He leaned back on the camp stool and slowly caressed the pewter-colored surface of his hair. "I decided a little walk might be in order for tomorrow night, after we secure the problem. Instead of going back to the base on the trucks. What do you think, Billy?"

"I think that's an excellent idea, sir. An excellent idea. In fact I've been meaning to suggest something like that to the Colonel for quite some time. As a means of inculcating a sort of group *esprit*."

"It's what they need, Billy."

"Full marching order, sir?" O'Leary put in seriously.

"No, that'd be a little rough."

"Aaa-h," O'Leary said, relieved.

Suddenly Culver heard Mannix's voice: "Even so—"

"Even so, what?" the Colonel interrupted. Again, the voice was not hostile, only anticipatory, as if it already held the answer to whatever Mannix might ask or suggest.

"Well, even so, Colonel," Mannix went on mildly, while Culver, suddenly taut and concerned, held

his breath, "even without packs thirty-six miles is
a long way for anybody, much less for guys who've
gone soft for the past five or six years. I'll admit
my company isn't the hottest outfit in the world,
but most of them are reserves—"

"Wait a minute, Captain, wait a minute," the
Colonel said. Once more the voice—as cool and as
level as the marshy ground upon which they were
sitting—carefully skirted any tone of reproach and
was merely explicit: "I don't want you to think I'm
taking it out on the Battalion merely because of
you, or rather H & S Company. But they aren't reserves. They're *marines. Comprend?*" He arose
from the chair. "I think," he went on flatly, almost
gently, "that there's one thing that we are all tend-
ing to overlook these days. We've been trying to
differentiate too closely between two particular
bodies of men that make up the Marine Corps.
Technically it's true that a lot of these new men
are reserves—that is, they have an 'R' affixed at the
end of the 'USMC.' But it's only a technical difference, you see. Because first and foremost they're
marines. I don't want my marines doping off.
They're going to *act* like marines. They're going
to be *fit.* If they meet an Aggressor enemy next
week they might have to march a long, long way.
And that's what I want this hike to teach them.
Comprend?" He made what could pass for the
token of a smile and laid his hand easily and for
a lingering second on Mannix's shoulder, in a sort
of half-gesture of conciliation, understanding—
something—it was hard to tell. It was an odd
picture because from where he sat Culver was the
only one in the tent who could see, at the same

19

instant, both of their expressions. In the morbid, comfortless light they were like classical Greek masks, made of chrome or tin, reflecting an almost theatrical disharmony: the Colonel's fleeting grin sculpted cleanly and prettily in the unshadowed air above the Captain's darkened, downcast face where, for a flicker of a second, something outraged and agonized was swiftly graven and swiftly scratched out. The Colonel's smile was not complacent or unfriendly. It was not so much as if he had achieved a triumph but merely equilibrium, had returned once more to that devout, ordered state of communion which the Captain's words had ever so briefly disturbed. At that moment Culver almost liked the Colonel, in some negative way which had nothing to do with affection, but to which "respect," though he hated the word, was the nearest approach. At least it was an honest smile, no matter how faint. It was the expression of a man who might be fatuous and a ham of sorts, but was not himself evil or unjust—a man who would like to overhear some sergeant say, "He keeps a tight outfit, but he's straight." In men like Templeton all emotions—all smiles, all anger—emanated from a priestlike, religious fervor, throbbing inwardly with the cadence of parades and booted footfalls. By that passion rebels are ordered into quick damnation but simple doubters sometimes find indulgence—depending upon the priest, who may be one inclined toward mercy, or who is one ever rapt in some litany of punishment and court-martial. The Colonel was devout but inclined toward mercy. He was not a tyrant, and his smile was a sign that the Captain's doubts were forgiven, prob-

ably even forgotten. But only Culver had seen the
Captain's face: a quick look of both fury and suffering, like the tragic Greek mask, or a shackled
slave. Then Mannix flushed. "Yes, sir," he said.

The Colonel walked toward the door. He seemed
already to have put the incident out of his mind.
"Culver," he said, "if you can ever make radio
contact with Able Company tell them to push off at
0600. If you can't, send a runner down before dawn
to see if they've got the word." He gave the side of
his thigh a rather self-conscious, gratuitous slap.
"Well, good night."

There was a chorus of "Good night, sirs," and
then the Major went out, too, trailed by O'Leary.
Culver looked at his watch: it was nearly three
o'clock.

Mannix looked up. "You going to try and get
some sleep, Tom?"

"I've tried. It's too cold. Anyway, I've got to
take over the radio watch from Junior here. What's
your name, fellow?"

The boy at the radio looked up with a start,
trembling with the cold. "McDonald, sir." He was
very young, with pimples and a sweet earnest expression; he had obviously just come from boot
camp, for he had practically no hair.

"Well, you can shove off and get some sleep,
if you can find a nice warm pile of pine needles
somewhere." The boy sleepily put down his earphones and went out, fastening the blackout flap
behind him.

"I've tried," Culver repeated, "but I just can't
get used to sleeping on the ground any more. I'm
getting old and rheumatic. Anyway, the Old Rock

was in here for about two hours before you came, using up my sack time while he told the Major and O'Leary and me all about his Shanghai days."

"He's a son of a bitch." Mannix morosely cupped his chin in his hands, blinking into space, at the bare canvas wall. He was chewing on the butt of a cigar. The glare seemed to accentutate a flat Mongoloid cast in his face; he looked surly and tough and utterly exhausted. Shivering, he pulled his field jacket closer around his neck, and then, as Culver watched, his face broke out into the comical, exasperated smile which always heralded his bitterest moments of outrage—at the Marine Corps, at the system, at their helpless plight, the state of the world—tirades which, in their unqualified cynicism, would have been intolerable were they not always delivered with such gusto and humor and a kind of grisly delight. "Thirty ... six ... *miles*," he said slowly, his eyes alive and glistening, "*thirty ... six ... miles!* Christ on a crutch! Do you realize how far that is? Why that's as far as it is from Grand Central to Stamford, Connecticut! Why, man, I haven't walked a hundred consecutive yards since 1945. I couldn't go thirty-six miles if I were sliding downhill the whole way on a sled. And a *forced* march, mind you. You just don't stroll along, you know. That's like running. That's a regulation two-and-a-half miles per hour with only a ten-minute break each hour. So H & S Company is fouled up. So maybe it is. He can't take green troops like these and do that. After a couple of seven- or ten- or fifteen-mile conditioning hikes, maybe so. If they were young. And rested. Barracks-fresh. But this silly son of a bitch is going to have all these tired, flabby old men flapping around on the ground like a bunch of fish after the first two miles. Christ on a frigging crutch!"

"He's not a bad guy, Al," Culver said, "he's just a regular. Shot in the ass with the Corps. A bit off his nut, like all of them."

But Mannix had made the march seem menacing, there was no doubt about that, and Culver— who for the moment had been regarding the hike as a sort of careless abstraction, a prolonged evening's stroll—felt a solid dread creep into his bones, along with the chill of the night. Involuntarily, he shuddered. He felt suddenly unreal and disoriented, as if through some curious second sight or seventh sense his surroundings had shifted, ever so imperceptibly, into another dimension of space and time. Perhaps he was just so tired. Freezing marsh and grass instead of wood beneath his feet, the preposterous cold in the midst of summer, Mannix's huge distorted shadow cast brutishly against the impermeable walls by a lantern so sinister that its raging noise had the sound of a typhoon at sea— all these, just for an instant, did indeed contrive to make him feel as if they were adrift at sea in a dazzling, windowless box, ignorant of direction or of any points of the globe, and with no way of telling. What he had had for the last years—wife and child and home—seemed to have existed in the infinite past or, dreamlike again, never at all, and what he had done yesterday and the day before, moving wearily with this tent from one strange thicket to a stranger swamp and on to the green depths of even stranger ravine, had no sequence, like the dream of a man delirious with fever. All time and space seemed for a moment to be enclosed within the tent, itself unmoored and unhelmed upon a dark and compassless ocean.

And although Mannix was close by, he felt profoundly alone. Something that had happened that evening—something Mannix had said, or suggested, perhaps not even that, but only a fleeting look in the Captain's face, the old compressed look of torment mingled with seething outrage—something that evening, without a doubt, had added to the great load of his loneliness an almost intolerable burden. And that burden was simply an anxiety, nameless for the moment and therefore the more menacing. It was not merely the prospect of the hike. Exhaustion had just made him vulnerable to a million shaky, anonymous fears—fears which he might have resisted had he felt strong and refreshed, or younger. His age was showing badly. All this would have been easy at twenty-three. But he was thirty, and seventy-two virtually sleepless hours had left him feeling bushed and defeated. And there was another subtle difference he felt about his advanced age—a new awakening, an awareness—and therein lay the reason for his fears.

It was simply that after six years of an ordered and sympathetic life—made the more placid by the fact that he had assumed he had put war forever behind him—it was a shock almost mystically horrifying, in its unreality, to find himself in this new world of frigid nights and blazing noons, of disorder and movement and fanciful pursuit. He was insecure and uprooted and the prey of many fears. Not for days but for weeks, it seemed, the battalion had been on the trail of an invisible enemy who always eluded them and kept them pressing on—across swamps and blasted fields and past indolent, alien streams. This enemy was labeled Aggressor, on maps brightly spattered with arrows and symbolic tanks and guns, but although there was no sign of his aggression he fled them nonetheless and they pushed the sinister chase, sending up shells and flares as they went. Five hours' pause, five hours in a tent somewhere, lent to the surrounding grove of trees a warm, homelike familiarity that was almost like permanence, and he left each command post feeling lonely and uprooted, as they pushed on after the spectral foe into the infinite strangeness of another swamp or grove. Fatigue pressed down on his shoulders like strong hands, and he awoke in the morning feeling weary, if he ever slept at all. Since their constant movement made the sunlight come from ever-shifting points of the compass, he was often never quite sure—in his steady exhaustion—whether it was morning or afternoon. The displacement and the confusion filled him with an anxiety which would not have been possible six years before, and increased his fatigue. The tent itself, in its tiny, momentary permanence, might have had all of the appeal of the home which he so desperately hungered for, had it not been so cold, and had it not seemed, as he sat there suddenly shivering with fear, so much more like a coffin instead.

Then it occurred to him that he was actually terrified of the march, of the thirty-six miles: not because of the length—which was beyond comprehension—but because he was sure he'd not be able to make it. The contagion of Mannix's fear had touched him. And he wondered then if Mannix's fear had been like his own: that no matter what his hatred of the system, of the Marine Corps, might be, some instilled, twisted pride would make him walk until he dropped, and his fear was not of the hike itself, but of dropping. He looked up at Mannix and said, "Do you think you can make it, Al?"

Mannix heavily slapped his knee. He seemed not to have heard the question. The giddy sensation passed, and Culver got up to warm his hands at the lamp.

"I'll bet if Regiment or Division got wind of this they'd lower the boom on the bastard," Mannix said.

"They have already. They said fine."

"What do you mean? How do you know?"

"He said so, before you came in. He radioed to the base for permission, or so he said."

"The bastard."

"He wouldn't dare without it," Culver said. "What I can't figure out is why Regiment gave him the O.K. on it."

"The swine. The little swine. It's not on account of H & S Company. You know that. It's because it's an exploit. He wants to be known as a tough guy, a boondocker."

"There's one consolation, though," said Culver, after a pause, "if it'll help you any."

"What, for God's sake?"

"Old Rocky, or whatever they call him, is going to hike along, too."

"You think so?" Mannix said doubtfully.

"I know so. So do you. He wouldn't dare not push along with his men."

Mannix was silent for a moment. Then he said viciously, as if obsessed with the idea that no act of Templeton's could remain untainted by a prime and calculated evil: "But the son of a bitch! He's made for that sort of thing. He's been running around the boondocks for six years getting in shape while sane people like you and me were home living like humans and taking it easy. Billy Lawrence, too. They're both gung ho. These fat civilians can't take that sort of thing. My God! Hobbs! Look at that radioman, Hobbs. That guy's going to keel over two minutes out—" He rose suddenly to his feet and stretched, his voice stifled by the long, indrawn breath of a yawn. "Aaa-h, fuck it. I'm going to hit the sack."

"Why don't you?"

"Fine bed. A poncho in a pile of poison ivy. My ass looks like a chessboard from chigger bites. Jesus, if Mimi could see me now." He paused and pawed at his red-rimmed eyes. "Yeah," he said, blinking at his watch, "I think I will." He slapped Culver on the back, without much heartiness. "I'll see you tomorrow, sport. Stay loose." Then he lumbered from the tent, mumbling something: *be in for fifty years.*

Culver turned away from the lamp. He sat down at the field desk, strapping a black garland of wires and earphones around his skull. The wild, lost wail of the radio signal struck his ears, mingling with the roar, much closer now, of the lamp; alone as he was, the chill and cramped universe of the tent seemed made for no one more competent than a blind midget, and was on the verge of bursting with a swollen obbligato of demented sounds. He felt almost sick with the need for sleep and, with the earphones still around his head, he thrust his face into his arms on the field desk. There was nothing on the radio except the signal; far off in the swamp the companies were sleeping wretchedly in scattered squads and platoons, tumbled about in the cold and the dark, and dreaming fitful dreams. The radios were dead everywhere, except for their signals: a crazy, tortured multitude of wails on which his imagination played in exhaustion. They seemed like the cries of souls in the anguish of hell, if he concentrated closely enough, shrill cracklings, whines, barks and shrieks—a whole jungle full of noise an inch from his eardrum and across which, like a thread of insanity, was strung the single faint fluting of a dance-band clarinet—blown in from Florida or New York, someplace beyond reckoning. His universe now seemed even more contained: not merely by the tiny space of the tent, but by the almost tangible fact of sound. And it was impossible to sleep. Besides, something weighed heavily on his mind; there was something he had forgotten, something he was supposed to do....

Then suddenly he remembered the Colonel's instructions. He cleared his throat and spoke drowsily into the mouthpiece, his head still resting against his arms. "This is Bundle Three calling Bundle Able. This is Bundle Three calling Bundle Able. This is Bundle Three calling Bundle Able. Do you hear me? Over ..." He paused for a moment, waiting. There was no answer. He repeated:

"This is Bundle Three calling Bundle Able, this is Bundle Three calling Bundle Able, this is..." And he snapped abruptly erect, thinking of Mannix, thinking: to hell with it: simply because the words made him feel juvenile and absurd, as if he were reciting Mother Goose.

He *would* stay awake. And he thought of Mannix. Because Mannix would laugh. Mannix appreciated the idiocy of those radio words, just as in his own crazy way he managed to put his finger on anything which might represent a symbol of their predicament. Like the radio code. He had a violent contempt for the gibberish, the boy-scout passwords which replaced ordinary conversation in the military world. To Mannix they were all part of the secret language of a group of morons, morons who had been made irresponsibly and dangerously clever. He had despised the other side, also—the sweat, the exertion, and the final danger. It had been he, too, who had said, "None of this Hemingway crap for me, Jack"; he was nobody's lousy hero, and he'd get out of this outfit some way. Yet, Culver speculated, who really was a hero anyway, any more? Mannix's disavowal of faith put him automatically out of the hero category, in the classical sense, yet if suffering was part of the hero's role, wasn't Mannix as heroic as any? On his shoulder there was a raw, deeply dented, livid scar, made the more conspicuous and, for that matter, more ugly, by the fact that its evil slick surface only emphasized the burly growth of hair around it. There were smaller scars all over his body. About them Mannix was neither proud nor modest, but just frank and once while they were showering

29

down after a day in the field, Mannix told him
how he had gotten the scars, one day on Peleliu.
"I was a buck sergeant then. I got pinned down in
a shell hole out in front of my platoon. Christ
knows how I got there but I remember there was
a telephone in the hole and—whammo!—the Nips
began laying in mortar fire on the area and I
got a piece right here." He pointed to a shiny,
triangular groove just above his knee. "I remember grabbing that phone and hollering for them
to for Christ's sake get the 81s up and knock out
that position, but they were slow, Jesus they were
slow! The Nips were firing for effect, I guess, because they were coming down like rain and every
time one of the goddam things went off I seemed
to catch it. All I can remember is hollering into
that phone and the rounds going off and the zing-
ing noise that shrapnel made. I hollered for 81s and
I caught a piece in my hand. Then I hollered for
at least a goddam rifle grenade and I caught a
piece in the ass, right here. I hollered for 60s and
guns and airplanes. Every time I hollered for
something I seemed to catch some steel. Christ, I
was scared. And hurting! Jesus Christ. I never hurt
so much in my life. Then I caught this one right
here"—he made a comical, contorted gesture, with
a bar of soap, over his shoulder—"man, it was lights
out then. I remember thinking, 'Al, you've had it,'
and just before I passed out I looked down at that
telephone. You know, that frigging wire had been
blasted right out of sight all that time."

No, perhaps Mannix wasn't a hero, any more
than the rest of them, caught up by wars in which,
decade by half-decade, the combatant served peon-

age to the telephone and the radar and the thunderjet—a horde of cunningly designed, and therefore often treacherous, machines. But Mannix had suffered once, that "once" being, in his own words, "once too goddam many, Jack." And his own particular suffering had made him angry, had given him an acute, if cynical, perception about their renewed bondage, and a keen nose for the winds that threatened to blow up out of the oppressive weather of their surroundings and sweep them all into violence. And he made Culver uneasy. His discontent was not merely peevish; it was rocklike and rebellious, and thus this discontent seemed to Culver to be at once brave and somehow full of peril.

He had first seen Mannix the revolutionary five months ago, soon after they had been called back to duty. He hadn't known him then. There were compulsory lectures arranged at first, to acquaint the junior officers with recent developments in what had been called "the new amphibious doctrine." The outlines of these lectures were appallingly familiar: the stuffy auditorium asprawl with bored lieutenants and captains, the brightly lit stage with its magnified charts and graphs, the lantern slides (at which point, when the lights went out, it was possible to sneak a moment's nap, just as in officers' school seven years ago), the parade of majors and colonels with their maps and pointers, and their cruelly tedious, doggedly memorized lectures: the whole scene, with its grave, professorial air, seemed seedily portentous, especially since no one cared, save the majors and colonels, and no one listened. When Culver sat down, during the darkness of a lantern slide, next to the big relaxed mass which he dimly identified as a captain, he noticed that it was snoring. When the lights went up, Mannix still slept on, filling the air around him with a loud, tranquil blubber. Culver aroused him with a nudge. Mannix grumbled something, but then said, "Thanks, Jack." A young colonel had come onto the stage then. He had made many of the lectures that week. He had a curiously thick, throaty voice which would have made him sound like a yokel, except that his words were coolly, almost passionately put, and he bent forward over the lectern with a bleak and solemn attitude—a lean, natty figure with hair cut so close to his head that he appeared to be, from that distance, nearly bald. "An SS man," Mannix whispered, "he's gonna come down here and cut your balls off. You Jewish?" He grinned and collapsed back, forehead against his hand, into quiet slumber. Culver couldn't recall what the colonel talked about: the movement of supplies, logistics, ship-to-shore movement, long-range planning, all abstract and vast, and an ardent glint came to his eyes when he spoke of the "grandiose doctrine" which had been formulated since they, the reserves, had been away. "You bet your life, Jack," Mannix had whispered out of the shadows then. He seemed to have snapped fully awake and, following the lecture intently, he appeared to address his whispers not to Culver, or the colonel, but to the air. "You bet your life they're grandiose," he said, "even if you don't know what grandiose means. I'll bet you'd sell your soul to be able to drop a bomb on somebody." And then, aping the colonel's instructions to the corporal—one of the enlisted flunkies, who, after each lecture, passed out the reams of

printed and mimeographed tables and charts and
résumés, which everyone promptly, when out of
sight, threw away—he whispered in high, throaty,
lilting mockery: "Corporal, kindly pass out the atom
bombs for inspection." He smacked the arm of his
seat, too hard; it could be heard across the auditorium, and heads turned then, but the colonel
had not seemed to have noticed. "Jesus," Mannix
rumbled furiously, "Jesus Christ almighty," while
the colonel droned on, in his countrified voice: "Our
group destiny," he said, "amphibiously integrated,
from any force thrown against us by Aggressor
enemy."

Later—toward the end of that week of lectures,
after Mannix had spoken the calm, public mani-
festo which at least among the reserves had made
him famous, and from then on the object of a
certain awe, though with a few doubts about his
balance, too—Culver had tried to calculate how
he had gotten by with it. Perhaps it had to do
with his size, his bearing. There was at times a
great massive absoluteness in the way he spoke.
He was huge, and the complete honesty and candor
of his approach seemed to rumble forth, like notes
from a sounding board, in direct proportion to his
size. He had suffered, too, and this suffering had
left a persistent, unwhipped, scornful look in his
eyes, almost like a stain, or rather a wound, which
spells out its own warning and cautions the un-
wary to handle this tortured parcel of flesh with
care. And he was an enormous man, his carriage
was formidable. That skinny, bristle-haired colonel,
Culver finally realized, had been taken aback past
the point of punishment, or even reprimand, mere-

ly because of the towering, unavoidable, physical
fact that he was facing not a student or a captain
or a subordinate, but a stubborn and passionate man.
So it was that, after a lecture on transport of supplies, when the colonel had called Mannix's name
at random from a list to answer some generalized,
hypothetical question, Mannix had stood up and
said merely, "I don't know, sir." A murmur of surprise passed over the auditorium then, for the colonel, early in the hour, had made it plain that he had
wanted at least an attempt at an answer—a guess—
even though they might be unacquainted with the
subject. But Mannix merely said, "I don't know, sir,"
while the colonel, as if he hadn't heard correctly,
rephrased the question with a little tremor of an-
noyance. There was a moment's silence and men
turned around in their seats to look at the author of
this defiance. "I don't know, sir," he said again, in a
loud but calm voice. "I don't know what my first
consideration would be in making a space table like
that. I'm an infantry officer. I got an 0302." The colonel's forehead went pink under the glare of the
lights. "I stated earlier, Captain, that I wanted some
sort of answer. None of you gentlemen is expected
to know this subject pat, but you can essay *some
kind of an answer*." Mannix just stood there, solid
and huge, blinking at the colonel. "I just have to re-
peat, sir," he said finally, "that I don't have the
faintest idea what my first consideration would be.
I never went to cargo-loading school. I'm an 0302.
And I'd like to respectfully add, sir, if I might, that
there's hardly anybody in this room who knows that
answer, either. They've forgotten everything they
ever learned seven years ago. Most of them don't

even know how to take an M-1 apart. They're too old. They should be home with their families." There was passion in his tone but it was controlled and straightforward—he had managed to keep out of his voice either anger or insolence—and then he fell silent. His words had the quality, the sternness, of an absolute and unequivocal fact, as if they had been some intercession for grace spoken across the heads of a courtroom by a lawyer so quietly convinced of his man's innocence that there was no need for gesticulations or frenzy. The colonel's eyes bulged incredulously at Mannix from across the rows of seats, but in the complete, astounded hush that had followed he was apparently at a loss for words. A bit unsteadily, he called out another name and Mannix sat down, staring stonily ahead.

It had been perhaps a court-martial offense, at least worthy of some reprimand, but that was all there was to it. Nothing happened, no repercussions, nothing. The thing had been forgotten; either that, or it had been stored away in the universal memory of colonels, where all such incidents are sorted out for retribution, or are forgotten. Whatever effect it had on the colonel, or whatever higher, even more important sources got wind of it, it had its effect on Mannix. And the result was odd. Far from giving the impression that he had been purged, that he had blown off excess pressure, he seemed instead more tense, more embittered, more in need to scourge something—his own boiling spirit, authority, anything.

Culver's vision of him at this time was always projected against Heaven's Gate, which was the name—no doubt ironically supplied at first by the enlisted men—of the pleasure-dome ingeniously erected amid a tangle of alluvial swampland, and for officers only. He and Mannix lived in rooms next to each other, in the bachelor quarters upstairs. The entire area was a playground which had all the casual opulence of a Riviera resort and found its focus in the sparkling waters of a swimming pool, set like an oblong sapphire amid flowered walks and a fanciful growth of beach umbrellas. There, at ten minutes past four each day, Mannix could be found, his uniform shed in an instant and a gin fizz in his hand—a sullen, mountainous figure in a lurid sportshirt, across which a squadron of monstrous butterflies floated in luminous, unmilitary files. Both Mannix and Culver hated the place—its factitious luxury, its wanton atmosphere of alcohol and torpid ease and dances, the vacant professional talk of the regular officers and the constant teasing presence of their wives, who were beautiful and spoke in tender drawls and boldly flaunted at the wifeless reserves—in a proprietary, Atlanta-debutante fashion—their lecherous sort of chastity. The place seemed to offer up, like a cornucopia, the fruits of boredom, of footlessness and dissolution. It was, in Mannix's words, like a prison where you could have anything you wanted except happiness, and once, in a rare midnight moment when he allowed himself to get drunk, he got paper and wood together from his room and announced to Culver in an unsteady but determined voice that he was going to burn the place down. Culver held him off, but it was true: they were bound to the pleasures of the place by necessity—for there was no place to go for a hundred miles, even if they had wanted to go—

and therefore out of futility. "Goddam, it's degrading," Mannix had said, making use of an adjective
which indeed seemed to sum it all up. "It's like sex
now. Or the lack of it. Now maybe it's all right for a
kid to go without sex, but it's degrading for someone like me almost thirty to go without making love
for so long. It's simply degrading, that's all. I'd go
for one of these regulars' pigs if it wasn't for Mimi.
. . . This whole mess is degrading. I know it's my
own fault I stayed in the reserves, Jack, you don't
have to tell me that. I was a nut. I didn't know I
was going to get called out for every frigging
international incident that came along. But, goddam, it's degrading"—and with a glum, subdued
gesture he'd down the dregs of his drink—"it's
degrading for a man my age to go sniffing around
on my belly in the boondocks like a dog. And
furthermore—" He looked scornfully about him, at
the glitter and chrome, at the terrace by the pool
where Japanese lanterns hung like a grove of pastel
moons, and a girl's shrill and empty laugh uncoiled
as bright as tinsel through the sluggish coastal dusk.
It was a silent moment in a night sprinkled with a
dusty multitude of Southern stars, and the distant
bleating saxophone seemed indecisive and sad, like
the nation and the suffocating summer, neither at
peace nor at war. "Furthermore, it's degrading to
come out of the field each day and then be *forced*
to go to a night club like this, when all you want
to do is go home to your wife and family. Goddam,
man, I've *gotta* get out!"

But underneath his rebellion, Culver finally
knew, Mannix—like all of them—was really resigned. Born into a generation of conformists, even

Mannix (so Culver sensed) was aware that his gestures were not symbolic, but individual, therefore hopeless, maybe even absurd, and that he was trapped like all of them in a predicament which one personal insurrection could, if anything, only make worse. "You know," he said once, "I think I was really afraid just one time last war." The phrase "last war" had had, itself, a numb, resigned quality, in its lack of any particular inflection, like "last week end," or "last movie I went to see." They had been lying on the beach to which they fled each hot week end. In that setting of coast and sea and lugubrious solitude they felt nearly peaceful, in touch with a tranquil force more important, and more lasting (or so it seemed on those sunlit afternoons), than war. Mannix had been, almost for the first time since Culver had known him, rested and subdued, and the sound of his voice had been a surprise after long, sun-laden hours of sleep and silence. "That's the goddam truth," he said thoughtfully, "I was only afraid once. Really afraid, I mean. It was at a hotel in San Francisco. I think I really came closer to dying that night than I ever have in my life. We were drunk, you see, polluted, all of us. I think there were five of us, all of us boots just out of Dago. Kids. We were on the tenth floor of this hotel and in this room and I believe we were about as drunk as anyone could get. I remember going in to take a shower in the bathroom. It was late at night, past midnight, and after I took this shower, you see, I came out into the room buck naked. Two of those drunk guys were waiting for me. They grabbed me and pushed me toward the window. I was so loaded I couldn't

battle. Then they pushed me out the window and
held me by the heels while I dangled upside-down
buck naked in space, ten floors above the street."
He paused and sucked at a beer can. "Can you
imagine that?" he went on slowly. "How I felt?
I got stone-sober in a second. Imagine being that
high upside-down in space with two drunks holding
onto your heels. I was heavy, man, just like now,
you see. All I can remember is those teeny-weeny
lights below and the tiny little people like ants
down there and those two crazy drunk guys holding
onto my wet slippery ankles, laughing like hell and
trying to decide whether to let go or not. I just
remember the cold wind blowing on my body and
that dark, man, infinite darkness all around me, and
my ankles beginning to slip out of their hands. I
really saw Death then, and I think that all I could
think of was that I was going to fall and smash
myself on that hard, hard street below. That those
crazy bastards were going to let me fall. I was
praying, I guess. I remember the blood rushing
to my brain and my ankles slipping, and that awful
strange noise. And I was reaching out, man, clutching at thin air. Then I wondered what that noise
was, that high loud noise, and then I realized it
was me, screaming at the top of my voice, all over
San Francisco." He stopped talking then and scuffed
at the sand with one calloused heel. "They hauled
me up somehow. It was those sober guys—I guess
they were sober—the other two. They got me up.
But every time I remember that moment a great
big cold shudder runs up and down my spine."
He chuckled and chewed on his cigar but the laugh
was half-hearted and listless, and he dug his elbows

into the sand and resumed his quiet, placid gaze toward the horizon. Culver watched him: his bitterness dissolved in the hot salty air, slumped in the sand gazing wistfully out to sea, sun-glassed, hairychested, a cigar protruding from his face and a beer can warming in his hand, he seemed no longer the man who could sicken himself with resentment, but relaxed, pliable even, like a huge hairy baby soothed by the wash of elemental tides, ready to receive anything, all into that great void in his soul which bitterness and rebellion had briefly left vacant—all—the finality of more suffering, or even death. War was in the offing. A promenade of waves, snow-crowned like lovely garlands in the dark hair of girls, swelled eastward toward Africa: past those smoky heights, more eastward still, the horizon seemed to give back repeated echoes of the sea, like far-off thunder, or guns. Culver remembered making a quick, contorted motion in the sand with his body, and being swept by a hot wave of anguish. It was loneliness and homesickness, but it was also fright. Across the rim of his memory two little girls playing on the sunny grass waved to him, were gone, pursued by a shower of uncapturable musical sounds. Mannix's resigned silence fed his loneliness. Suddenly he felt, like Mannix, upturned drunkenly above the abyss, blood rushing to his head, in terror clutching at the substanceless night. . . .

In the noonday light Sergeant O'Leary, his face brightly pink, was still talking. Culver snapped awake with a start. O'Leary grinned down at him— "Damn, Lieutenant, you're gonna crap out tonight if you're that tired now"—and Culver struggled for speech; time seemed to have unspooled past him in a great spiral, and for an instant—his mind still grappling with the memory of a hurried, chaotic nightmare—he was unable to tell where he was. He had the feeling that it should be the night before, and that he was still in the tent. "Did I go to sleep, O'Leary?" he said, blinking upward.

"Yes, sir," O'Leary said, and chuckled, "you sure did."

"How long?"

"Oh, just a second."

"Christ, I *am* tired. I dreamt it was last night," Culver said. He got to his feet. A truck moved through the clearing in a cloud of dust. There seemed to be new activity in the command post, and new confusion. Culver and O'Leary turned together then toward the operations tent; the Colonel had come out and was striding toward them, followed by Mannix.

"Culver, get your jeep and driver," he said, walking toward the road, not looking up. His voice was briskly matter-of-fact; he strode past them with short, choppy steps and the swagger stick in his hand made a quick tattoo, *slap-slap*-slapping against his dungaree pants. "I want you and Captain Mannix to go with me down to Third Batt. See if we can help." His voice faded; Mannix trailed behind him, saying nothing, but his face seemed to Culver even more exhausted, and even more grimly taut, than it had been an hour before.

The road was a dusty cart-path that rambled footlessly across scrubby, fallow farmland. Shacks and cabins, long ago abandoned, lay along its way.

They piled into the jeep, Mannix and Culver in the back, the Colonel in front next to the driver. They hadn't far to go—less than a mile—but the trip felt endless to Culver because the day, by now a fitful carrousel of sleepy sounds, motions without meaning, seemed wildly, almost dangerously abstracted, as if viewed through drug-glazed eyes or eyes, like those of a mole, unacquainted with light. Dust billowed past them as they went. Above them a blue cloudless sky in which the sun, pitched now at its summit, beat fearfully down, augured no rain for the day, or for the evening. Mannix said nothing; his silence prompted Culver to turn and look at him. He was gazing straight ahead with eyes that seemed to bore through the Colonel's neck. Tormented beast in the cul-de-sac, baffled fury, a grief at the edge of defeat—his eyes made Culver suddenly aware of what they were about to see, and he turned dizzily away and watched the wreck of a Negro cabin float past through the swirling dust: shell-shattered doors and sagging walls, blasted facade—a target across which for one split second in the fantastic noon there seemed to crawl the ghosts of the bereaved and the departed, mourning wraiths come back to reclaim from the ruins some hot scent of honeysuckle, smell of cooking, murmurous noise of bees. Culver closed his eyes and drowsed, slack-jawed, limp, his stomach faintly heaving.

One boy's eyes lay gently closed, and his long dark lashes were washed in tears, as though he had cried himself to sleep. As they bent over him they saw that he was very young, and a breeze came up from the edges of the swamp, bearing with it a

scorched odor of smoke and powder, and touched
the edges of his hair. A lock fell across his brow
with a sort of gawky, tousled grace, as if preserving
even in that blank and mindless repose some gesture
proper to his years, a callow charm. Around his
curly head grasshoppers darted among the weeds.
Below, beneath the slumbering eyes, his face had
been blasted out of sight. Culver looked up and
met Mannix's gaze. The Captain was sobbing helplessly. He cast an agonized look toward the Colonel,
standing across the field, then down again at the
boy, then at Culver. "Won't they ever let us alone,
the sons of bitches," he murmured, weeping. "Won't
they ever let us alone?"

THREE

That evening at twilight, just before the beginning
of the march, Mannix found a nail in his shoe.
"Look at it," he said to Culver, "what lousy luck."
They were sitting on an embankment bordering the
road. The blue dusk was already scattered with
stars, but evening had brought no relief to the heat
of the day. It clung to them still, damp and stifling,
enveloping them like an overcoat. The battalion,
over a thousand men, was ready for the march.
It stretched out in two files on either side of the
road below them for more than a mile. Culver
turned and looked down into Mannix's shoe; sure
enough, a nail-end had penetrated the lining at the
base of the heel, a sharp pinpoint of torture. Mannix inspected the bottom of his big dirty foot. He
pulled off a flake of skin which the nail had already
worn away. "Of all the lousy luck," he said, "gimme
a Band-Aid."

"It'll wear right through, Al," Culver said, "you'd

better get another pair of shoes. Try flattening it
out with the end of your bayonet."

Mannix hammered for a moment at the nail and
then looked up in exasperation. "It won't go all the
way. Gimme that Band-Aid." A rusty spatter of
blood he had picked up at noon and still on the
sleeve of his dungarees. He had become nervous and
touchy. All that afternoon, after they had come back,
he had seemed, like Culver, still shaken by the
slaughter, still awed, and rather despondent. Finally,
he had alternated moments of remote abstraction
with quick outbursts of temper. The shock of the explosion seemed to have set something off in him. His
mood had become vague and unpredictable, and he
was able to shift from sour, uncommunicative gloom
to violent anger in an instant. Culver had never
seen him quite so cranky before, nor had he ever
seen him so testily at odds with his men, to whom
he usually had shown the breeziest good will. All
afternoon he'd been after them, nagging, bellowing
orders—only to fall suddenly into a profound and
brooding silence. As he squatted in the weeds eating his evening meal two hours before, he had
hardly said a word, except to murmur—irrelevantly,
Culver thought—that his company "had better goddam well shape up." It puzzled Culver; the explosion seemed to have stripped off layers of skin from
the Captain, leaving only raw nerves exposed.

Now he had become fretful again, touchily alert,
and his voice was heavy with impatience. He mum-
bled as he plastered the Band-Aid on his foot. "I
wish they'd get this show on the road. That's the
trouble with the Marine Corps, you always stand
frigging around for half the night while they think

45

up some grandiose doctrine. I wish to Christ I'd
joined the Army. Man, if I'd known what I was
getting in for when I went down to that recruiting
office in 1941, I'd have run off at the door." He
looked up from his foot and down toward the command group nearly at the head of the column. Three
or four officers were clustered together on the road.
The Colonel was among them, neat, almost jaunty,
in new dungarees and boots. On his head there was
a freshly clean utility cap with a spruce uptilted
bill and a shiny little silver leaf. At his side he wore
a pearlhandled .38 revolver, glistening with silver
inlay. It was, as usual, loaded, though no one knew
why, for he was never known to shoot it; the general
feeling seemed to be that it was his emblematic
prerogative, no more an affectation, certainly, than a
visored hat encrusted with gilt, or grenades worn at
the shoulder. The pistol—like the swagger stick; the
nickname; the quizzical, almost tenderly contemplative air of authority—was part of the act, and to be
sure, Culver reflected, the act was less offensive, less
imperious than it might be. One simply learned soon
to believe that the pistol "belonged," just as the
name "Old Rocky" belonged; if such an act finally
did no harm, if it only flattered his vanity, was the
Colonel to be blamed, Culver asked himself, if he
did nothing to mitigate the total impression?

Mannix watched him, too, watched the Colonel
toe at the sand, thumbs hooked rakishly in his belt,
a thin gentle smile on his face, adumbrated by the
fading light: he looked youthful and fresh, non-
chalant, displaying the studied casualness of an
athlete before the stadium throng, confident of his
own victory long before the race begins. Mannix

gnawed at the end of a cigar, spat it out viciously. "Look at the little jerk. He thinks he's gonna have us pooped out at the halfway mark—"

Culver put in, "Look Al, why don't you do something about that nail? If you told the Colonel he'd let you ride in—"

Mannix went fiercely on, in a husky whisper: "Well he's not. He's a little sadist, but he's not gonna have Al Mannix crapped out. I'll walk anywhere that son of a bitch goes and a mile further. He thinks H & S Company's been doping off. Well, I'll show him. I wouldn't ask him to ride in if I'd been walking over broken glass. I'll—"

He paused. Culver turned and looked at him. They were both silent, staring at each other, embarrassed by the common understanding of their gaze. Each turned away; Mannix murmured something and began to tie his shoe. "You're right, Al," Culver heard himself saying. It seemed it was almost more than he could bear. Night was coming on. As in a stupor, he looked down the road at the battalion, the men lounging along the embankments with their rifles, smoking and talking in tired, subdued voices, smoke rising in giant blue clouds through the dusk, where swarms of gnats rose and fell in vivacious, panicky flight. In the swamp, frogs had begun a brainless chorale; their noise seemed perfectly suited to his sense of complete and final frustration. It was almost more than he could bear. So Mannix had felt it, too: not simply fear of suffering, nor exhaustion, nor the lingering horror, which gripped both of them, of that bloody wasteland in the noonday heat. But the other; the old atavism that clutched them, the voice that commanded, once

47

again, *you will*. How stupid to think they had ever made their own philosophy; it was as puny as a house of straw, and at this moment—by the noise in their brains of those words, *you will*—it was being blasted to the winds like dust. They were as helpless as children. Another war, and years beyond reckoning, had violated their minds irrevocably. For six years they had slept a cataleptic sleep, dreaming blissfully of peace, awakened in horror to find that, after all, they were only marines, responding anew to the old commands. They were marines. Even if they were old. Bank clerks and salesmen and lawyers. Even if, right now, they were unutterably tired. They could no more *not* be determined to walk the thirty-six miles than they could, in the blink of an eye, turn themselves into beautiful nymphs. Culver was afraid he wasn't going to make it, and now he knew Mannix was afraid, and he didn't know what to feel—resentment or disgust—over the fact that his fear was mingled with a faint, fugitive pride.

Mannix looked up from his shoe and at the Colonel. "You're goddam right, Jack, we're going to make it," he said. "My company's going to make it if I have to *drag in their bodies*." There was a tone in his voice that Culver had never heard before.

Suddenly the Colonel's flat voice broke through the stillness: "All right, Billy, let's saddle up."

" 'Tallion saddle up!" The Major's words were eager and shrill, became multiplied down the long mile. "Smoking lamps out!" The blue cloud dissolved on the air, the gnats descended in a swarm and the voices passed on—*Saddle up, saddle up*— while the battalion rose to its feet, not all at once but in a steady gradual surge, like rows of corn snapping back erect after the passing of a wind. Mannix got to his feet, began to sideslip in a cloud of dust down the embankment toward his company directly below. It was at the head of the column, right behind the command group. Culver, moving himself now down the hill, heard Mannix's shout. It rang out in the dusk with deliberate authority, hoarse blunt command: "All right, H & S Company, saddle up, saddle up! You people get off your asses and straighten up!" Culver passed by him on his way to the command group: he stood surrounded by a cloud of gnats, hulking enormously above the company, hands balanced lightly on his hips, poised forward badgering the men like some obsessed, rakehell Civil War general before a battle: "All right, you people, we're gonna walk thirty-six miles tonight and I mean walk! First man I see drop out's gonna get police duty for two weeks, and that goes for everybody. You think I'm kidding you wait and see. There's gonna be trucks going in for those that can't make it but I don't want to see anyone from H & S Company climbing on! If an old man with as much flab as I've got can make it you people can too. . . ." There was a note, almost, of desperation in his voice. Culver, passing along the line of bedraggled, mournful-looking men, so few of whom looked like fabled marines, heard the voice rise to a taut pitch close to frenzy; it was too loud, it worried Culver, and he wished to caution him: no longer just admonishing the men to a simple duty, it was the voice of a man wildly fanatic with one idea: to last. "I want to hear no bitching out of you people! Take it easy on the water. You get shin-

splints or blisters you see the corpsman, don't come
crying to me. When we get in I want to see all of
you people. ..." Not because the hike was good
or even sensible, Culver thought, but out of hope
of triumph, like a chain-gang convict who endures
a flogging without the slightest whimper, only to
spite the flogger. Culver joined the command group,
heard the Colonel say to the Major: "Looks like
H & S Company's going to make it *en masse*, Billy."
It was just as Culver feared, for although his words
were pleasant enough, his face, regarding Mannix
for a brief moment, had a look of narrow scrutiny,
as if he, too, had detected in the Captain's tone that
note of proud and willful submission, rebellion in
reverse. But there was no emotion in his voice as he
turned quickly, with a glance at his watch, and said,
"Let's move out, Billy."

They started out without delay. A jeep, its headlamps lit, preceded them. The Colonel, in the lead,
abreast of the Major and just ahead of Culver,
plunged off into the deep dust of the road. He
walked with a slinky-hipped, athletic stride, head
down between his shoulders and slightly forward,
arms bent and moving methodically; nothing broke
the rhythm of his steps—ruts in the road or the
deeply grooved tire tracks—and Culver became
quickly amazed, and rather appalled, at the pace
he was setting. It was the pace of a trained hiker—
determined, unhesitant, much closer to a trot now
than a walk—and only a few minutes passed before
Culver was gasping for breath. Sand lay thick in
the road, hindering a natural step. They had not
gone more than a couple of hundred yards; already
he felt sweat trickling down his forehead and be-

neath his arms. For a moment fear surged up in him
unnaturally, and a crazy panic. He had been afraid
of the march before, but his fear had been abstract
and hazy; now so quickly fatigued, in what seemed
a matter of seconds, he felt surely (as Mannix had
predicted) that he'd be unable to last the first hour.
A panicky wash of blood came to his face and he
struggled for breath, wanting to cry out—it passed.
His mind groped for reason and the terror receded:
once he adjusted to the shock of this pace, he realized, he'd be all right. Then the panic went away;
as it did so, he found himself breathing easier, freed
of that irrational fright. The Colonel pushed ahead
in front of him with the absolute mechanical con-
fidence of a wound-up, strutting tin soldier on a
table top. Culver, panting a bit, heard his voice,
as calm and unwinded as if he were sitting at a desk
somewhere, addressed to the Major: "We shoved
off at nine on the dot, Billy. We should make the
main road at ten and have a break." "Yes, sir," he
heard the Major say, "we'll be ahead of the game."
Culver made a calculation then; by the operations
map, which he knew so well, that was three and a
half miles—a mile farther than the regulation distance for an hour's march. It was, indeed, like running. Pushing on through the sand, he felt a wave
of hopelessness so giddy and so incomprehensible
that it was almost like exhilaration—and he heard
a noise—half-chuckle, half-groan—escape between
his labored breaths. Three and a half miles: the
distance from Greenwich Village almost to Harlem.
In his mind he measured that giddy parade of city
blocks, an exhausting voyage even on wheels. It
was like twisting a knife in his side but he went

51

on with the mental yardstick—to imagine himself
plodding that stretch up the sandless, comfortably
receptive pavements of Fifth Avenue, past Four-
teenth Street and the bleak vistas of the Twenties
and the Thirties, hurrying onward north by the Li-
brary, twenty blocks more to the Plaza, and pressing
still onward along the green acres of the Park ... his
thoughts recoiled. Three and a half miles. In an
hour. With more than thirty-two still to go. A vision
of Mannix came swimming back; Culver stumbled
along after the dauntless Colonel, thinking, Christ
on a crutch.

They hastened on. Night had fallen around them,
tropic and sudden, lit now, as they descended across
a thicket of swampy ground, only by the lights of
the jeep. Culver had regained his wind but already
his chest and back were awash in sweat, and he
was thirsty. He took a vague comfort in the fact
that others felt the same way, for behind him he
heard canteens being unsnapped from their cases,
rattling out of their cups, and the noise, in mid-
march, of drinking—a choked, gurgling sound—
then, faint to the rear, Mannix's angry voice: "All
right, goddammit, I told you people to hold onto
your water! Put those goddam canteens back until
the break!" Culver, craning his neck around, saw
nothing—no Mannix, who had apparently dropped
behind—nothing except a shadowy double line of
men laboring through the sand, fading off far down
the road into the general blackness. To the rear
some marine made a joke, a remark; there was
laughter and a snatch of song—*on top of old
Smo-oky, all covered* ... Then Mannix's voice again
out of the dark: "O.K. you people can grabass all

52

you want but I'm telling you you'd better save your wind. If you want to talk all the way it's O.K. with me but you're gonna crap out if you do, and remember what I said. . . ." His tone had become terse and vicious; it could have been the sound of a satrap of Pharaoh, a galley master. It had the forbidding quality of a strand of barbed wire or a lash made of thorns, and the voices, the song, abruptly ceased, as if they had been strangled. Still his words continued to sting and flay them—already, in this first hour, with the merciless accents of a born bully—and Culver, suddenly angered, had an impulse to drop back and try to make him let up.

"You people close it up now! Dammit, Shea, keep those men closed up there. They fall back they're gonna have to run to catch up! Goddammit, close it up now, you hear me! I mean *you*, Thompson, goddammit you aren't deaf! Close it up! *Close it up*, I said!" So it was that the voice, brutal and furious, continued the rest of the way.

And so it was that those first hours Culver recollected as being the most harrowing of all, even though the later hours brought more subtle refinements of pain. He reasoned that this was because during the first few miles or so he was at least in rough possession of his intellect, his mind lashing his spirit as pitilessly as his body. Later, he seemed to be involved in something routine, an act in which his brain, long past cooperation, played hardly any part at all. But during these early hours there was also the fact of Mannix. Superimposed upon Culver's own fantasies, his anger, his despair (and his own calm moments of rationalization, too) was his growing awareness of what was happening to the Captain. Later, Mannix's actions seemed to become mixed up and a part of the general scheme, the nightmare. But here at first Culver's mind was enough in focus for Mannix's transformation to emerge clearly, even if with the chill, unreal outlines of coming doom—like a man conversing, who might turn around briefly to a mirror and see behind him in the room no longer his familiar friend, but something else—a shape, a ghost, a horror—a wild and threatful face reflected from the glass.

They made the highway at ten o'clock, almost to the minute. When the Colonel looked at his watch and stopped and the Major raised his arm, shouting, "Breather! Ten minutes!" Culver went over to the side of the road and sat down in the weeds. Blood was knocking angrily at his temples, behind his eyes, and he was thirsty enough to drink, with a greedy recklessness, nearly a third of his canteen. He lit a cigarette; it tasted foul and metallic and he flipped it away. His knees and thighs, unaccustomed to so much pounding, were stiff and fatigued; he stretched them out slowly into the dewy underbrush, looking upward at a placid cloud of stars. He turned. Up the road, threading its way through a barrier of outstretched legs and rifles, came a figure. It was Mannix. He was still muttering as he lumbered up and sank down beside him. "Those goddam people, they won't keep it closed up. I have to dog them every minute. They're going to find themselves running the whole way if they don't keep closed up. Gimme a butt." He was breathing heavily, and he passed the back of his hand over his brow to wipe the sweat away.

"Why don't you leave them alone?" Culver said. He gave the Captain a cigarette, which he lit, blowing the smoke out in a violent sort of choked puff.

"Dammit," he replied, coughing, "you *can't* leave them alone! They don't want to make this lousy hike. They'd just as soon crap out on the side and let the trucks haul them in. They'd just as soon take police duty. Man, they're reserves. They don't care who sees them crap out—me, anybody." He fell back with a sigh into the weeds, arms over his eyes. "Fuck it," he said. Culver looked down at him. From the jeep's headlamps an oblong of yellow slanted across the lower part of his face. One corner of his mouth jerked nervously—a distasteful grimace, as if he had been chewing something sour. Exhausted, completely bushed, there was something in his manner—even in repose—which refused to admit his own exhaustion. He clenched his teeth convulsively together. It was as if his own fury, his own obsession now, held up, Atlas-like, the burden of his great weariness. "Jesus," he murmured, almost irrelevantly, "I can't help thinking about those kids today, lying out there in the weeds."

Culver rested easily for a moment, thinking too. He looked at his watch, with a sinking sensation: six of their ten minutes had already passed—so swiftly that they seemed not to have existed at all. Then he said, "Well, for Christ's sake, Al, why don't you let them crap out? If you were getting screwed like these enlisted men are you'd crap out too, you wouldn't care. You don't have to chew them out like you've been doing. Let's face it, you don't really care if they make it. You. Me, maybe. But these guys . . . anybody else. What the hell." He paused, fumbling for words, went on feebly, *"Do you?"*

Mannix rose up on his elbows then. "You're damn right I do," he said evenly. They turned toward the Colonel standing not far away; he and the Major, pointing a flashlight, were bent together over a map. Mannix hawked something up and spat. His voice became more controlled. "You see that little jerk standing there?" he said. "He thinks he's pulling something on us. Thirty-six miles. *No-*body walks that far, stateside. *No*body. We never walked that far even with Edson, last war. See, that little jerk wants to make a name for himself—Old Rocky Templeton. Led the longest forced march in the history of the Corps—"

"But—" Culver started.

"He'd just love to see H & S crap out," he went on tensely, "he'd *love* it. It'd do something to his ego. Man, I can see him now"—and his voice lifted itself in a tone of sour mockery—" 'Well, Cap'n Mannix, see where you had a little trouble last night getting your men in. Need a little bit more *esprit*, huh?' " His voice lowered, filled with venom. "Well, screw *him*, Jack. I'll get my company in if I have to carry them on my back—"

It was useless to reason with him. Culver let him go on until he had exhausted his bitter spurt of hatred, of poison, and until finally he lay back again with a groan in the weeds—only a moment before the cry came again: "Saddle up! Saddle up!"

They pushed off once more. It was just a bit easier now, for they were to walk for two miles on

the highway, where there was no sand to hinder
their steps, before turning back onto the side roads.
Yet there was a comfortless feeling at the outset,
too: legs cramped and aching from the moment's
rest, he walked stooped and bent over, at the start,
like an arthritic old man, and he was sweating again,
dry with thirst, after only a hundred yards. How
on earth, he wondered, gazing up for a second at
the dim placid landscape of stars, would they last
until the next morning, until nearly noon? A car
passed them—a slick convertible bound for the
North, New York perhaps—wherever, inevitably,
for some civilian pleasure—and its fleet, almost
soundless passage brought, along with the red pinpoint of its vanishing taillights, a new sensation of
unreality to the night, the march: dozing, shrouded
by the dark, its people seemed unaware of the
shadowy walkers, had sped unceasingly on, like
ocean voyagers oblivious of all those fishy struggles
below them in the night, submarine and fathomless.

They plodded on, the Colonel pacing the march,
but slower now, and Culver played desperately
with the idea that the man would, somehow, tire,
become exhausted himself. A wild fantasia of hopes
and imaginings swept through his mind: that Templeton *would* become fatigued, having overesti-
mated his own strength, *would* stop the march after
an hour or so and load them on the trucks—like a
stern father who begins a beating, only to become
touched with if not remorse then leniency, and
stays his hand. But Culver knew it was a hollow desire. They pushed relentlessly ahead, past
shadowy pine groves, fields dense with the fragrance
of alfalfa and wild strawberries, shuttered farm-

houses, deserted rickety stores. Then this brief
civilized vista they abandoned again, and for good,
when without pause they plunged off again onto
another road, into the sand. Culver had become
bathed in sweat once more; they all had, even the
Colonel, whose neat dungarees had a black triangular wet spot plastered at their back. Culver heard
his own breath coming hoarsely again, and felt the
old panic: He'd never be able to make it, he knew,
he'd fall out on the side like the old man he was—
but far back to the rear then he heard Mannix's
huge voice, dominating the night: "All right, goddammit, move out! We got sand here now. Move
out and close it up, I say, goddammit! Leadbetter,
get that barn out of your ass and close it up! *Close
it up,* I say!" They spurred Culver on, after a fashion, but following upon those shouts, there was a
faint, subdued chorus, almost inaudible, of moans
and protests. They came only from Mannix's company, a muffled, sullen groan. To them Culver heard
his own fitful breath add a groan—expressing something he could hardly put a name to: fury, despair,
approaching doom—he scarcely knew. He stumbled
on behind the Colonel, like a ewe who follows the
slaughterhouse ram, dumb and undoubting, too
panicked by the general chaos to hate its leader, or
care.

At the end of the second hour, and three more
miles, Culver was sobbing with exhaustion. He
flopped down in the weeds, conscious now of a
blister beginning at the bottom of his foot, as if it
had been scraped by a razor.

Mannix was having trouble, too. This time when
he came up, he was limping. He sat down silently

and took off his shoes; Culver, gulping avidly at his canteen, watched him. Both of them were too winded to smoke, or to speak. They were sprawled beside some waterway—canal or stream; phosphorescent globes made a spooky glow among shaggy Spanish moss, and a rank and fetid odor bloomed in the darkness—not the swamp's decay, Culver realized, but Mannix's feet. "Look," the Captain muttered suddenly, "that nail's caught me right in the heel." Culver peered down by the glare of Mannix's flashlight to see on his heel a tiny hole, bleeding slightly, bruised about its perimeter and surrounded by a pasty white where the Band-Aid had been pulled away. "How'm I going to do it with that?" Mannix said.

"Try beating that nail down again."

"I tried, but the point keeps coming out. I'd have to take the whole frigging shoe apart."

"Can't you put a piece of cloth over it or something?"

"I tried that, too, but it puts my foot off balance. It's worse than the nail." He paused. "Jesus Christ."

"Look," Culver said, "try taking this strip of belt and putting it over it." They debated, operated, talked hurriedly, and neither of them were aware of the Colonel, who had walked over through the shadows and was standing beside them. "What's the matter, Captain?" he said.

They looked up, startled. Hands hooked as usual —Culver wanted to say "characteristically"—in his belt, he stood serenely above them. In the yellow flashlight glow his face was red from exertion, still damp with sweat, but he appeared no more fatigued than a man who had sprinted a few yards to catch

a bus. The faint smile hovered at the corners of his
lips. Once more it was neither complacent nor su-
perior but, if anything, almost benevolent, so that
by the unnatural light, in which his delicate features became fiery red and again now, along the
borders of his slim tapering fingers, nearly trans-
parent, he looked still not so much the soldier but
the priest in whom passion and faith had made an
alloy, at last, of only the purest good intentions;
above meanness or petty spite, he was leading a
march to some humorless salvation, and his smile—
his solicitous words, too—had at least a bleak sin-
cerity.

"I got a nail in my shoe," Mannix said.

The Colonel squatted down and inspected Mannix's foot, cupping it almost tenderly in his hand.
Mannix appeared to squirm at the Colonel's touch.
"That looks bad," he said after a moment, "did you
see the corpsman?"

"No, sir," Mannix replied tensely, "I don't think
there's anything can be done. Unless I had a new
pair of boondockers."

The Colonel ruminated, rubbing his chin, his
other hand still holding the Captain's foot. His eyes
searched the dark reaches of the surrounding
swamp, where now the rising moon had laid a tranquil silver dust. Fogs piped shrilly in the night,
among the cypress and the shallows and closer now,
by the road and the stagnant canal, along which
danced shifting pinpoints of fire—cigarettes that
rose and fell in the hidden fingers of exhausted men.
"Well," the Colonel finally said, "well—" and paused.
Again the act—: indecision before decision, the

waiting. "Well," he said and paused again. The waiting. At that moment—in a wave that came up through his thirst, his throbbing lips, his numb sense of futility—Culver felt that he knew of no one on earth he had ever loathed so much before. And his fury was heightened by the knowledge that he did not hate the man—the Templeton with his shrewd friendly eyes and harmless swagger, that fatuous man whose attempt to convey some impression of a deep and subtle wisdom was almost endearing— not this man, but the Colonel, the marine: that was the one he despised. He didn't hate him for himself, nor even for his brutal march. Bad as it was, there were no doubt worse ordeals; it was at least a peaceful landscape they had to cross. But he did hate him for his perverse and brainless gesture: squatting in the sand, gently, almost indecently now, stroking Mannix's foot, he had too long been conditioned by the system to perform with grace a human act. Too ignorant to know that with this gesture—so nakedly human in the midst of a crazy, capricious punishment which he himself had imposed—he lacerated the Captain by his very touch. Then he spoke. Culver knew what he was going to say. Nothing could have been worse.

"Well," he said, "maybe you'd better ride in on one of the trucks."

If there had been ever the faintest possibility that Mannix would ride in, those words shattered it. Mannix drew his foot away abruptly, as if the Colonel's hand were acid, or fire. "No, sir!" he said fiercely—too fiercely, the note of antagonism, now, was unmistakable—"No, sir! I'll make this frigging march." Furiously, he began to put on his shoe. The Colonel rose to his feet, hooked his thumbs in his belt and gazed carelessly down.

"I think you're going to regret it," he said, "with that foot of yours."

The Captain got up, limping off toward his company, over his retreating shoulder shot back a short, clipped burst of words at the Colonel—whose eyeballs rolled white with astonishment when he heard them—and thereby joined the battle.

"Who cares what you think," he said.

FOUR

Had the Colonel entertained any immediate notions
of retribution, he held them off, for at a quarter
past four that morning—halfway through the march,
when the first green light of dawn streaked the sky
—Culver still heard Mannix's hoarse, ill-tempered
voice, lashing his troops from the rear. For hours he
had lost track of Mannix. As for the Colonel, the
word had spread that he was no longer pacing the
march but had gone somewhere to the rear and was
walking there. In his misery, a wave of hope swelled
up in Culver: if the Colonel had become fagged,
and was walking no longer but sitting in his jeep
somewhere, at least they'd all have the consolation
of having succeeded while their leader failed. But
it was a hope, Culver knew, that was ill-founded.
He'd be back there slogging away. The bastard
could outmarch twenty men, twenty raging Man-
nixes.

The hike had become disorganized, no slower

but simply more spread out. Culver—held back by
fatigue and thirst and the burning, enlarging pain
in his feet—found himself straggling behind. From
time to time he managed to catch up; at one point
he discovered himself at the tail end of Mannix's
company, but he no longer really cared. The night
had simply become a great solitude of pain and
thirst, and an exhaustion so profound that it en-
veloped his whole spirit, and precluded thought.

A truck rumbled past, loaded with supine marines, so still they appeared unconscious. Another
passed, and another—they came all night. But far
to the front, long after each truck's passage, he
could hear Mannix's cry: "Keep on, Jack! This company's walking in." They pushed on through the
night, a shambling horde of zombies in drenched
dungarees, eyes transfixed on the earth in a sort of
glaze, avid concentration. After midnight it seemed
to Culver that his mind only registered impressions,
and these impressions had no sequence but were
projected upon his brain in a scattered, disordered
riot, like a movie film pieced together by an idiot.
His memory went back no further than the day
before; he no longer thought of anything so unat-
tainable as home. Even the end of the march
seemed a fanciful thing, beyond all possibility, and
what small aspirations he now had were only to
endure this one hour, if just to attain the micro-
scopic bliss of ten minutes' rest and a mouthful of
warm water. And bordering his memory was ever
the violent and haunting picture of the mangled
bodies he had seen—when? where? it seemed
weeks, years ago, beneath the light of an almost
prehistoric sun; try as he could, to dwell upon con-

soling scenes—home, music, sleep—his mind was balked beyond that vision: the shattered youth with slumbering eyes, the blood, the swarming noon.

Then at the next halt, their sixth—or seventh, eighth, Culver had long ago lost count—he saw Mannix lying beside a jeep-towed water-cart at the rear of his company. O'Leary was sprawled out next to him, breath coming in long asthmatic groans. Culver eased himself painfully down beside them and touched Mannix's arm. The light of dawn, a feverish pale green, had begun to appear, outlining on Mannix's face a twisted look of suffering. His eyes were closed.

"How you doing, Al?" Culver said, reaching up to refill his canteen.

"Hotsy-totsy," he breathed, "except for my frigging foot. How you making it, boy?" His voice was listless. Culver looked down at Mannix's shoe; he had taken it off, to expose heel and sock, where, soaked up like the wick of a lantern, rose a dark streak of blood.

"Jesus," Culver said, "Al, for Christ sake now, you'd better ride in on a truck."

"Nail's out, sport. I finally stole me a pair of pliers, some radioman. Had to run like hell to catch up."

"Even so—" Culver began. But Mannix had fallen into an impervious silence. Up the road stretched a line of squatting men, Mannix's company. Most were sprawled in the weeds or the dust of the road in attitudes as stiff as death, yet some nearby sat slumped over their rifles, drinking water, smoking; there was a thin resentful muttering in the air. And the men close at hand—the faces he could see in the indecisive light—wore looks of agonized and silent protest. They seemed to be mutely seeking for the Captain, author of their misery, and they were like faces of men in bondage who had jettisoned all hope, and were close to defeat. In the weeds Mannix breathed heavily, mingling his with the tortured wheezes of O'Leary, who had fallen sound asleep. It was getting hot again. No one spoke. Then a fitful rumbling filled the dawn, grew louder, and along the line bodies stirred, heads turned, gazed eastward down the road at an oncoming, roaring cloud of dust. Out of the dust came a machine. It was a truck, and it passed them, and it rattled to a stop up in the midst of the company.

"Anyone crapped out here?" a voice called. "I got room for ten more."

There was a movement toward the truck; nearby, half a dozen men got to their feet, slung their rifles, and began to hobble up the road. Culver watched them tensely, hearing Mannix stir beside him, putting his shoe back on. O'Leary had awakened and sat up. Together the three of them watched the procession toward the truck: a straggle of limping men plodding as wretchedly as dog-pound animals toward that yawning vehicle in the smoky dawn, huge, green, and possessed of wheels—which would deliver them to freedom, to sleep, oblivion. Mannix watched them without expression, through inflamed eyes; he seemed so drugged, so dumb with exhaustion, that he was unaware of what was taking place. "What happened to the Colonel?" he said absently.

"He went off in a jeep a couple of hours ago,"

O'Leary said, "said something about checking on the column of march."

"What?" Mannix said. Again, he seemed unaware of the words, as if they—like the sight of this slow steaming exodus toward the truck—were making no sudden imprint on his mind, but were filtering into his consciousness through piles and layers of wool. A dozen more men arose and began a lame procession toward the truck. Mannix watched them, blinking. "What?" he repeated.

"To check the column, sir," O'Leary repeated. "That's what he said."

"He *did?*" Mannix turned with an angry, questioning look. "Who's pacing the march, then?"

"Major Lawrence is."

"He *is?*" Mannix rose to his feet, precariously, stiffly and in pain balancing himself not on the heel, but the toe only, of his wounded foot. He blinked in the dawn, gazing at the rear of the truck and the cluster of marines there, feebly lifting themselves into the interior. He said nothing and Culver, watching him from below, could only think of the baffled fury of some great bear cornered, bloody and torn by a foe whose tactics were no braver than his own, but simply more cunning. He bit his lips—out of pain perhaps, but as likely out of impotent rage and frustration, and he seemed close to tears when he said, in a tone almost like grief: "*He* crapped out! *He* crapped out!"

He came alive like a somnambulist abruptly shocked out of sleep, and he lunged forward onto the road with a wild and tormented bellow. "Hey, you people, get off that goddam truck!" He sprang into the dust with a skip and a jump, toiling down the road with hobbled leg and furious flailing arms. By his deep swinging gait, his terrible limp, he looked no more capable of locomotion than a wheel-chair invalid, and it would have been funny had it not seemed at the same time so full of threat and disaster. He pressed on. "Off that truck, goddammit, I say! Off that truck. Saddle up. Saddle up now, I say! On your feet!" he yelled. "Get off that goddam truck before I start kicking you people in the ass!" His words flayed and cowed them; a long concerted groan arose in the air, seemed to take possession of the very dawn; yet they debarked from the truck in terrified flight, scuttling down like mice from a sinking raft. "Move the hell out of here!" he shouted at the truck driver, a skinny corporal, eyes bulging, who popped back into the cab in fright. "Get that heap out of here!" The truck leaped off with a roar, enveloping the scene in blue smoke and a tornado of dust. Mannix, with windmilling arms, stood propped on his toe in the center of the road, urged the men wildly on. "Saddle up now! Let somebody else crap out O.K., but not you people, hear me! Do you hear me! Goddammit, I mean it! Shea, get those people moving out up there! You people better face it, you got eighteen more miles to go. ..." Culver tried to stop him, but they had already begun to run.

Panic-stricken, limping with blisters and with ex-haustion, and in mutinous despair, the men fled west-ward, whipped on by Mannix's cries. They pressed into the humid, sweltering light of the new day. Culver followed; O'Leary, without a murmur, puffed along beside him, while to the rear, with steady slogging footsteps, trailed the remnants of the battalion. Dust billowed up and preceded them, like Egypt's pillar of cloud, filling the air with its dry oppressive menace. It coated their lips and moist brows with white powdery grit, like a spray of plaster, and gave to the surrounding trees, the underbrush and vacant fields, a blighted pallor, as if touched by unseasonable frost. The sun rose higher, burning down at their backs so that each felt he bore on his shoulders not the burden of a pack but, almost worse, a portable oven growing hotter and hotter as the sun came up from behind the sheltering pines. They walked automatically, no longer with that light and tentative step in order to ease the pain in their feet, but with the firm, dogged tread of robots; and if they were all like Culver they had long since parted with a sensation of motion below the hips, and felt there only a constant throbbing pain—of blisters and battered muscles and the protest of exhausted bones.

Then one time Culver saw the Colonel go by in a jeep, boiling along in a cloud of dust toward the head of the column. He caught a glimpse of him as he passed: he looked sweaty and tired, far from rested, and Culver wondered how justified Mannix's outrage had been, assigning to the Colonel that act of cowardice. So he hadn't been pacing the march, but God knows he must have been hiking along to the rear; and his doubts were bolstered by O'Leary's voice, coming painfully beside him: "Old Captain Mannix's mighty pissed off at the Colonel." He paused, wheezing steadily. "Don't know if he's got a right to be that way. Old Colonel ain't gonna crap out without a reason. Colonel's kind of rough sometimes but he'll go with the troops." Culver said

nothing. They plodded ahead silently. Culver felt
like cursing the Sergeant. How could he be so stupid? How could he, in the midst of this pain, yield
up still only words of accord and respect and even
admiration for the creator of such a wild and lunatic
punishment? Only a man so firmly cemented to the
system that all doubts were beyond countenance
could say what O'Leary did—and yet—and yet God
knows, Culver thought wearily, he could be right
and himself and Mannix, and the rest of them, in-
escapably wrong. His mind was confused. A swarm
of dust came up and filled his lungs. Mannix was
screwing everything up horribly, and Culver wanted
suddenly to sprint forward—in spite of the effort it
took—reach the Captain, take him aside and tell
him: *Al, Al, let up, you've already lost the battle.*
Defiance, pride, endurance—none of these would
help. He only mutilated himself by this perverse
and violent rebellion; no matter what the Colonel
was—coward and despot or staunch bold leader—
he had him beaten, going and coming. Nothing
could be worse than what Mannix was doing—adding to a disaster already ordained (Culver somehow
sensed) the burden of his vicious fury. At least let
up, the men had had enough. But his mind was
confused. His kidneys were aching as if they had
been pounded with a mallet, and he walked along
now with his hands on his waist, like a professor
lecturing in a classroom, coattails over his arms.

And for the first time he felt intolerably hot—
with a heat that contributed to his mounting fury.
At night they had sweated more from exertion; the
coolness of the evening had been at least some
solace, but the morning's sun began to flagellate him

anew, adding curious sharp blades of pain to the
furious frustration boiling inside him. Frustration
at the fact that he was not independent enough, nor
possessed of enough free will, was not *man* enough
to say to hell with it and crap out himself; that he
was not man enough to disavow all his determination and endurance and suffering, cash in his chips,
and by that act flaunt his contempt of the march,
the Colonel, the whole bloody Marine Corps. But he
was *not* man enough, he knew, far less simply a free
man; he was just a marine—as was Mannix, and so
many of the others—and they had been marines, it
seemed, all their lives, would go on being marines
forever; and the frustration implicit in this thought
brought him suddenly close to tears. Mannix. A cold
horror came over him. Far down, profoundly, Mannix was so much a marine that it could make him
casually demented. The corruption begun years ago
in his drill-field feet had climbed up, overtaken
him, and had begun to rot his brain. Culver heard
himself sobbing with frustration and outrage. The
sun beat down against his back. His mind slipped
off into fevered blankness, registering once more,
on that crazy cinematic tape, chaos, vagrant jigsaw
images: Mannix's voice far ahead, hoarse and break-
ing now, then long spells of silence; halts beside
stifling, windless fields, then a shady ditch into
which he plunged, feverish and comatose, dreaming
of a carnival tent where one bought, from a dozen
barrels, all sorts of ice, chipped, crushed, and cubed,
in various shapes and sizes. He was awakened by
that terrible cry—*Saddle up, saddle up!*—and he
set out again. The sun rose higher and higher.
O'Leary, with a groan, dropped behind and van-

ished. Two trucks passed loaded with stiff, green-clad bodies motionless as corpses. The canteen fell off Culver's belt, somewhere, sometime; now he found though, to his surprise, that he was no longer thirsty and no longer sweating. This was dangerous, he recalled from some lecture, but at that moment the young marine vomiting at the roadside seemed more important, even more interesting. He stopped to help, thought better of it, passed on—through a strange crowd of pale and tiny butterflies, borne like bleached petals in shimmering slow-motion across the dusty road. At one point Hobbs, the radioman, cruised by in a jeep with a fishpole antenna; he was laughing, taunting the marchers with a song—*I got romance in my pants*—and he waved a jolly fat hand. A tanager rose, scarlet and beautiful, from a steaming thicket and pinwheeled upward, down again, and into the meadow beyond: there Culver thought, for a brief terrified moment, that he saw eight butchered corpses lying in a row, blood streaming out against the weeds. But it passed. Of course, he remembered, that was yesterday—or was it?—and then for minutes he tried to recall Hobbs' name, gave up the effort; it was along about this time, too, that he gazed at his watch, neither pleased nor saddened to find that it was not quite nine o'clock, began to wind it with careful absorption as he trudged along, and looked up to see Mannix looming enormously at the roadside.

"Get up," the Captain was saying. He had hardly any voice left at all; whatever he spoke with gave up only a rasp, a whisper. "Get your ass off the deck," he was saying, "get up, I say."

Culver stopped and watched. The marine lay

back in the weeds. He was fat and he had a three-
day growth of beard. He held up one bare foot,
where there was a blister big as a silver dollar and
a dead, livid white, the color of a toadstool; as the
Captain spoke, the marine blandly peeled the skin
away, revealing a huge patch of tender, pink, virgin
flesh. He had a patient hillbilly voice and he was
explaining softly, "Ah just cain't go on, Captain,
with a foot like this. Ah just cain't do it, and that's
all there is to it."

"You *can*, goddammit," he rasped. "I walked ten
miles with a nail in my foot. If I can do it you can,
too. Get up, I said. You're a marine. . . ."

"Captain," he went on patiently, "Ah cain't help
it about your nail. Ah may be a marine and all that
but Ah ain't no goddam fool. . . ."

The Captain, poised on his crippled foot, made
a swift, awkward gesture toward the man, as if to
drag him to his feet; Culver grabbed him by the
arm, shouting furiously: "Stop it, Al! Stop it! Stop
it! Stop it! Enough!" He paused, looking into Mannix's dull hot eyes. "Enough!" he said, more quietly.
"Enough." Then gently, "That's enough, Al. They've
just had enough." The end was at hand, Culver
knew, there was no doubt of that. The march had
come to a halt again, the men lay sprawled out on
the sweltering roadside. He looked at the Captain,
who shook his head dumbly and suddenly ran
trembling fingers over his eyes. "O.K.," he murmured, "yeah . . . yes"—something incoherent and
touched with grief—and Culver felt tears running
down his cheeks. He was too tired to think—except:
old Al. Mannix. Goddam. "They've had enough," he
repeated.

Mannix jerked his hand away from his face. "O.K.," he croaked, "Christ sake, I hear you. O.K. They've had enough, they've had enough. O.K. I heard you the first time. Let 'em crap out! I've did —done—" He paused, wheeled around. "To hell with them all."

He watched Mannix limp away. The Colonel was standing nearby up the road, thumbs hooked in his belt, regarding the Captain soberly. Culver's spirit sank like a rock. Old Al, he thought. You just couldn't win. Goddam. Old great soft scarred bear of a man.

If in defeat he appeared despondent, he retained one violent shred of life which sustained him to the end—his fury. It would get him through. He was like a man running a gauntlet of whips, who shouts outrage and defiance at his tormentors until he falls at the finish. Yet—as Culver could have long ago foretold—it was a fury that was uncontained; the old smoking bonfire had blazed up in his spirit. And if it had been out of control hours ago when he had first defied the Colonel, there was no doubt at all that now it could not fail to consume both of them. At least one of them. Culver, prone on his belly in the weeds, was hot with tension, and he felt blood pounding at his head when he heard the Colonel call, in a frosty voice: "Captain Mannix, will you come here a minute?"

Culver was the closest at hand. There were six more miles to go. The break had extended this time to fifteen minutes—an added rest because, as Culver had heard the Colonel explain to the Major, they'd walk the last six miles without a halt. Another break, he'd said, with a wry weary grin, and they'd never be able to get the troops off the ground. Culver had groaned—another senseless piece of sadism—then reasoned wearily that it *was* a good idea. Probably. Maybe. Who knew? He was too tired to care. He watched Mannix walk with an awful hobbling motion up the road, face screwed up in pain and eyes asquint like a man trying to gaze at the sun. He moved at a good rate of speed but his gait was terrible to behold—jerks and spasms which warded off, reacted to, or vainly tried to control great zones and areas of pain. Behind him most of his men lay in stupefied rows at the edge of the road and waited for the trucks to come. They knew Mannix had finished, and they had crumpled completely. For the last ten minutes, in a listless fashion, he had assembled less than a third of the company who were willing to continue the march —die-hards, athletes, and just those who, like Mannix himself, would make the last six miles out of pride and spite. Out of fury. It was a seedy, bedraggled column of people: of hollow, staring eyes and faces green with slack-jawed exhaustion; and behind them the remnants of the battalion made hardly more than two hundred men. Mannix struggled on up the road, approached the Colonel, and stood there propped on his toe, hands on his hips for balance.

The Colonel looked at him steadily for a moment, coldly. Mannix was no longer a simple doubter but the heretic, and was about to receive judgment. Yet there was still an almost paternal reluctance in Templeton's voice as he spoke, slowly and very softly, out of the troops' hearing: "Captain Mannix, I want you to go in on the trucks."

"No, sir," Mannix said hoarsely, "I'm going to make this march."

The Colonel looked utterly whipped; gray bags of fatigue hung beneath his eyes. He seemed no longer to have strength enough to display his odd theatrical smile; his posture was taut and vaguely stooped, the unmistakable bent-kneed stance of a man with blisters, and Culver was forced to concede —with a sense of mountainous despair—that he *had* made the march after all, somewhere toward the rear and for legitimate reasons of his own, even if Mannix now was too blind, too outraged, to tell. *Goddam,* Culver heard himself moaning aloud, *if just he only hadn't made it,* but he heard the Colonel go on coolly: "Not with that foot you aren't." He glanced down. The Captain's ankle had swollen to a fat milky purple above the top of his shoe; he was unable to touch his heel to the ground even if he had wanted to. "Not with that foot," he repeated.

Mannix was silent, panting deeply—not as if taken aback at all, but only as if gathering wind for an outburst. He and the Colonel gazed at each other, twin profiles embattled against an escarpment of pines, the chaste blue sky of morning. "Listen, Colonel," he rasped, "you ordered this goddam hike and I'm going to walk it even if I haven't got one goddam man left. You can crap out yourself for half the march—" Culver wanted desperately, somehow, by any means to stop him—not just because he was pulling catastrophe down on his head but because it was simply no longer worth the effort. Couldn't he see? That the Colonel didn't care and that was that? That with him the hike had had nothing to

do with courage or sacrifice or suffering, but was
only a task to be performed, that whatever he was
he was no coward, he had marched the whole way
—or most of it, any idiot could see that—and that
he was as far removed from the vulgar battle, the
competition, which Mannix had tried to promote as
the frozen, remotest stars. He just didn't care. Culver strove, in a sick, heaving effort, to rise, to go
and somehow separate them, but Mannix was
charging on: "You run your troops. Fine. O.K. But
what's all this about crapping out—"

"Wait a minute, Captain, now—" the Colonel
blurted ominously. "For your information—"

"*Fuck* you and your information," said Mannix
in a hoarse, choked voice. He was almost sobbing.
"If you think—"

But he went no further, for the Colonel had
made a curious, quick gesture—stage-gesture, fantastic and subtle, and it was like watching an old
cowboy film to see the Colonel's hand go swiftly
back to the handle of his pistol and rest there, his
eyes cool and passionate and forbidding. It was a
gesture of force which balked even the Captain.
Mannix's face went pale—as if he had only just then
realized the words which had erupted so heedlessly
from his mouth—and he said nothing, only stood
there sullen and beaten and blinking at the glossy
white handle of the pistol as the Colonel went on:
"For your information, Captain, you aren't the only
one who made this march. But I'm not *interested* in
your observations. You quiet down now, hear? You
march in, see? I order you confined to your quarters, and I'm going to see that you get a court-

martial. Do you understand? I'm going to have you
tried for gross insubordination. I'll have you sent to
Korea. *Keep your mouth shut.* Now get back to your
company!" He was shaking with wrath; the hot
morning light beat with piety and with vengeance
from his gray, outraged eyes. "Get back to your
men," he whispered, *"get back to your men!"*

Then he turned his back to the Captain and
called down the road to the Major: "All right, Billy,
let's saddle up!"

So it was over, but not quite all. The last six
miles took until past noon. Mannix's perpetual tread
on his toe alone gave to his gait a ponderous, bob-
bing motion which resembled that of a man wretchedly spastic and paralyzed. It lent to his face too—
whenever Culver became detached from his own
misery long enough to glance at him—an aspect
of deep, almost prayerfully passionate concentration
—eyes thrown skyward and lips fluttering feverish-
ly in pain—so that if one did not know he was in
agony one might imagine that he was a communi-
cant in rapture, offering up breaths of hot desire to
the heavens. It was impossible to imagine such a
distorted face; it was the painted, suffering face of
a clown, and the heaving gait was a grotesque and
indecent parody of a hopeless cripple, with shoulders gyrating like a see-saw and with flapping,
stricken arms. The Colonel and the Major had long
since out-distanced them, and Culver and Mannix
walked alone. When the base came into sight, he
was certain they were not going to make it. They
trudged into the camp. Along the barren, treeless
streets marines in neat khaki were going to lunch,
and they turned to watch the mammoth gyrating

Captain, so tattered and soiled—who addressed convulsive fluttering prayers to the sky, and had obviously parted with his senses. Then Mannix stopped suddenly and grasped Culver's arm. "What the hell," he whispered, "we've made it."

FIVE

For a long while Culver was unable to sleep. He
had lain naked on his bed for what seemed hours,
but unconsciousness would not come; his closed
eyes offered up only vistas of endless roads, steaming thickets, fields, tents—sunshine and darkness
illogically commingled—and the picture, which returned to his mind with the unshakable regularity
of a scrap of music, of the boys who lay dead beneath the light of another noon. Try as he could,
sleep would not come. So he dragged himself erect
and edged toward the window, laboriously, because
of his battered feet; it took him a full minute to do
so, and his legs, like those of an amputee which
possess the ghost of sensation, felt as if they were
still in motion, pacing endless distances. He lowered
himself into a chair and lighted a cigarette. Below,
the swimming pool was grotto-blue, a miniature of
the cloudless sky above, lit with shapes of dancing
light as shiny as silver dimes. A squad of sunsuited

maidens, officers' wives, splashed at its brink or ate ice-cream sundaes on the lawn, and filled the noontime with their decorous sunny laughter. It was hot and still. Far off above the pines, in the hot sunlight and over distant peace and civilization, brewed the smoky and threatful beginnings of a storm.

Culver let his head fall on his arm. Yes, they had had it—those eight boys—he thought, there was no doubt of that. In mindless slumber now, they were past caring, though diadems might drop or Doges surrender. They were ignorant of all. And that they had never grown old enough to know anything, even the tender miracle of pity, was perhaps a better ending—it was hard to tell. Faint warm winds came up from the river, bearing with them a fragrance of swamp and pine, and a last whisper of air passed through the trees, shuddered, died, became still; suddenly Culver felt a deep vast hunger for something he could not explain, nor ever could remember having known quite so achingly before. He only felt that all of his life he had yearned for something that was as fleeting and as incommunicable, in its beauty, as that one bar of music he remembered, or those lovely little girls with their ever joyful, ever sprightly dance on some far and fantastic lawn—serenity, a quality of repose—he could not call it by name, but only knew that, somehow, it had always escaped him. As he sat there, with the hunger growing and blossoming within him, he felt that he had hardly ever known a time in his life when he was not marching or sick with loneliness or afraid.

And so, he thought, they had all had it, in their various fashions. The Colonel had had his march

and his victory, and Culver could not say still why
he was unable to hate him. Perhaps it was only because he was a different kind of man, different
enough that he was hardly a man at all, but just a
quantity of attitudes so remote from Culver's world
that to hate him would be like hating a cannibal,
merely because he gobbled human flesh. At any
rate, he had had it. And as for Mannix—well, *he'd*
certainly had it, there was no doubt of *that*. Old Al,
he thought tenderly. The man with the back un-
breakable, the soul of pity—where was he now,
great unshatterable vessel of longing, lost in the
night, astray at mid-century in the never-endingness
of war?

His hunger faded and died. He raised his head
and gazed out the window. Over the pool a figure
swan-dived against the sky, in crucified, graceless
descent broke the water with a lumpy splash. A
cloud passed over the day, darkening the lawn with
a moment's somber light. The conversation of the
girls became subdued, civilized, general. Far off
above the trees, on the remotest horizon, thunder-
heads bloomed, a squall. Later, toward sundown,
they would roll landward over a shadowing reach
of waves, borne nearer, ever more darkly across the
coast, the green wild desolation of palmetto and
cypress and pine—and here, where the girls pink
and scanty in sunsuits would slant their tar-black
eyes skyward in the gathering night, abandon pool
and games and chatter and with shrill cries of warning flee homeward like gaudy scraps of paper on the
blast, voices young and lovely and lost in the darkness, the onrushing winds. One thing, Culver
thought, was certain—they were in for a blow. Al-

ready there would be signals up and down the coast.

Abruptly he was conscious of a dry, parched thirst. He rose to his feet, put on a robe, and hobbled out into the hallway toward the water cooler. As he rounded the corner he saw Mannix, naked except for a towel around his waist, making his slow and agonized way down the hall. He was hairy and enormous and as he inched his way toward the shower room, clawing at the wall for support, his face with its clenched eyes and taut, drawn-down mouth was one of tortured and gigantic suffering. The swelling at his ankle was the size of a grapefruit, an ugly blue, and this leg he dragged behind him, a dead weight no longer capable of motion.

Culver started to limp toward him, said, "Al—" in an effort to help him along, but just then one of the Negro maids employed in the place came swinging along with a mop, stopped, seeing Mannix, ceased the singsong little tune she was humming, too, and said, "Oh my, you poor man. What you been doin'? Do it hurt?" Culver halted.

"Do it hurt?" she repeated. "Oh, I bet it does. 'Deed it does." Mannix looked up at her across the short yards that separated them, silent, blinking. Culver would remember this: the two of them communicating across that chasm one unspoken moment of sympathy and understanding before the woman, spectacled, bandannaed, said again, "Deed it does," and before, almost at precisely the same instant, the towel slipped away slowly from Mannix's waist and fell with a soft plop to the floor; Mannix then, standing there, weaving dizzily and clutching for support at the wall, a mass of scars and naked as the day he emerged from his mother's womb, save for the soap which he held feebly in one hand. He seemed to have neither the strength nor the ability to lean down and retrieve the towel and so he merely stood there huge and naked in the slanting dusty light and blinked and sent toward the woman, finally, a sour, apologetic smile, his words uttered, it seemed to Culver, not with self-pity but only with the tone of a man who, having endured and lasted, was too weary to tell her anything but what was true.

" 'Deed it does," he said.

WILLIAM STYRON

WILLIAM STYRON was born in Newport News, Virginia, in 1925, and grew up in a nearby town listening to his grandmother's tales of her slave-owning days. His first story appeared in a student collection at Duke University, where he was a Marine officer candidate. Summoned to Okinawa, he arrived there, bearing the fresh stripes of a lieutenant, just as WWII was ending. Styron returned to Duke and graduated in 1947. Later that year he moved to New York and enrolled in Hiram Haydn's short story course at the New School. His work there became part of his first novel, LIE DOWN IN DARKNESS (1951), which brought him fame at the age of 26 when he was awarded the Prix de Rome by the American Academy of Arts and Letters. Shortly after, Styron moved to Paris, where he helped found, together with George Plimpton, Peter Matthiessen and Donald Hall, the *Paris Review*. Before travelling on to Rome, Styron wrote—in one intense six-week period during the summer of 1952 —THE LONG MARCH. His third novel, SET THIS HOUSE ON FIRE, based partly on Styron's journey to Italy, was published in 1960. Seven years later, he completed THE CONFESSIONS OF NAT TURNER—his brilliant and controversial portrayal of the historical Black revolutionist, which won the 1967 Pulitzer Prize. After a long literary silence, Styron emerged with another monumental work: SOPHIE'S CHOICE (1979), his impassioned and emotionally devastating novel of a Holocaust survivor, and one of the great critical and popular successes of recent years.

The Most Important Voices of Our Age

WINDSTONE BOOKS

This new line of books from Bantam brings you the most important voices and established writers of our age. Windstone. The name evokes the strong, enduring qualities of the air and the earth. The imprint represents the same qualities in literature—boldness of vision and enduring power, importance and originality of concept and statement. Windstone brings you contemporary masterpieces at affordable prices.

☐	22921	THE HILL OF EVIL COUNSEL Amos Oz	$2.95
☐	22741	A WOMAN OF THE FUTURE David Ireland	$3.95
☐	22603	THE REALMS OF GOLD Margaret Drabble	$3.95
☐	13476	WRINKLES Charles Simmons	$2.95
☐	20576	ALICE JAMES J. Strouse	$4.95
☐	23468	MIDDLE GROUND Margaret Drabble	$3.95
☐	20817	THE NEEDLE'S EYE Margaret Drabble	$3.95
☐	20575	HOUSEKEEPING Marilynne Robinson	$2.95
☐	14668	CONFESSIONS OF NAT TURNER William Styron	$3.95
☐	14705	GILES GOAT BOY John Barth	$4.95
☐	14704	DARKNESS VISIBLE William Golding	$3.95
☐	14667	THE LONG MARCH William Styron	$2.50
☐	14666	SET THIS HOUSE ON FIRE William Styron	$3.95
☐	20055	THE STONE ANGEL Margaret Laurence	$2.95

Prices and availability subject to change without notice.

Buy them at your local bookstore or use this handy coupon for ordering:

Windstone Books from Bantam bring you the most
important voices and established writers of our age.
They evoke the strong, enduring qualities of the air
and the earth. Here are more Windstone titles with
that same quality.

☐	23439	**THE KILLING GROUND** Mary Lee Settle	$3.95
☐	20184	**THE HOUSE ON PRAGUE STREET** Hana Demetz	$3.50
☐	23197	**AN UNKNOWN WOMAN: A JOURNEY** **TO SELF-DISCOVERY** Alice Koller	$3.95
☐	22604	**THE DIVINERS** M. Laurence	$3.95
☐	20850	**THE GOLDEN NOTEBOOK** D. Lessing	$4.95
☐	22817	**MEMOIRS OF A SURVIVOR** D. Lessing	$3.95
☐	20848	**AT PLAY IN THE FIELDS OF THE LORD** P. Matthiessen	$3.50
☐	20847	**FAR TORTUGA** P. Matthiessen	$3.95
☐	20665	**THE SNOW LEOPARD** P. Matthiessen	$3.95
☐	13441	**ONE DAY IN THE LIFE OF** **IVAN DENISOVICH** Alexander Solzhenitsyn	$2.50
☐	20647	**DELTA OF VENUS** Anais Nin	$3.50
☐	22969	**A SPY IN THE HOUSE OF LOVE** Anais Nin	$2.95
☐	13402	**LUNAR ATTRACTIONS** Clark Blaise	$3.95

Prices and availability subject to change without notice.

Bantam Books, Inc., Dept. WD6, 414 East Golf Road, Des Plaines, Ill. 60016

Please send me the books I have checked above. I am enclosing $_____
(please add $1.25 to cover postage and handling). Send check or money
order—no cash or C.O.D.'s please.

Mr/Mrs/Miss_____

Address _____

City_____State/Zip_____

WD6—10/83

Please allow four to six weeks for delivery. This offer expires 4/84.